THE
CHASE

To Alejandro

May all your dreams come true!

May

THE
CHASE

M. DAVID

Indigo River Publishing

Indigo River Publishing
3 West Garden Street Ste. 352 M
Pensacola, FL 32502
www.indigoriverpublishing.com

Book Design: mycustombookcover.com
Editor: Earl Tillinghast, Regina Cornell
Cover Photo Model: Braden Hendrickson

Ordering Information: Quantity sales: Special discounts are available on quantity purchases by corporations, associations, and others. For details, contact the publisher at the address above.

Orders by U.S. trade bookstores and wholesalers: Please contact the publisher at the address above.

Printed in the United States of America

Library of Congress Control Number: 2018947691

ISBN: 978-1-948080-35-4

First Edition

With Indigo River Publishing, you can always expect great books, strong voices, and meaningful messages. Most importantly, you'll always find ... words worth reading.

Dedication

I would like to dedicate this book to all those who want to make a difference in this world. Never let someone tell you "it can't be done"! Don't confuse mistakes with failures. Learning from your mistakes brings you closer to success. You are special and have the ability to do many wonderful things. Dreams can come true. You just have to believe it's possible!

CHAPTER ONE

"Quick, get up!" At first, I thought I was dreaming. I kept hearing it over and over: *"Quick, get up!"* I felt someone touching my shoulder. *"Wake up! You must get out now!"* I opened my eyes a crack. I could make out my dad's silhouette looming over me.

"What's wrong?" I asked, my voice still groggy with sleep. I opened my eyes a bit more. His face appeared gray in the darkened room. He kept saying that there was no time to talk. I was so confused. "What's going on?" I asked again, but he didn't answer. Now I was worried. Until two minutes ago, my dad was the calmest person in the world. He was a policeman, a detective, and nothing ever rattled him. Something bad had to be going down, very bad.

Dad went to my hockey bag and started dumping its contents on the floor. I watched as he dragged the bag to my dresser and started stuffing it with underwear, jeans, and tee shirts. "You have to hurry, there's not much time left!"

I reached over to turn on my bed lamp.

"No!" he shouted and yanked the lamp's cord from the outlet. "No light!"

He threw some clothes on the bed. "Get dressed, and don't worry about your hair."

Now I had something else to worry about: my hair! I did what he said. I pushed my legs through my jeans and pulled the shirt over my head.

"You'll need some money"—he reached into his back pocket, pulled out his wallet, and flipped it into the hockey bag—"and this, too." He scooped my Gameboy off my computer desk, wedged it between two tee shirts, and shoved it into the bag's side compartment. Grabbing my arm, he pushed me toward the window. "Go, go, *go!*" he shouted.

He opened the window and looked down. "You'll be okay. Just climb out, walk across the roof to the tree, and climb down. It's easy."

He must have seen the scared look on my face. Well, he was right, but it wasn't about walking across the roof and climbing down the tree. Heck, I'd done that over a billion times. I climbed out into the cold, damp night, being careful not to step on the wet leaves that were scattered on the sloping roof. I waited for him to climb through the window and join me on the roof ledge.

"Don't forget this," he said and pushed the hockey bag out the window instead.

"Aren't you coming?" I asked.

He just gave me a look and answered, "Don't worry about me."

In all the confusion, I hadn't realized something until just then. "Dad, where's Mom?"

I saw his eyes start to water. It took him a second to answer. "Don't worry about her. Please don't ask any more questions."

As I reached over to pick up the bag, he shoved a paper into my back pocket, placed his hand on my cheek, and said, "You have to go now, son. There's no time left. Get as far away as you can."

He closed the window and left me on the rooftop, alone in the cold, dreary night.

I strapped the bag to my back and carefully maneuvered around the wet leaves toward the tree. *This can't be happening*, I thought. I shivered slightly. The cold night air proved that I wasn't dreaming. I reached the old oak tree and climbed down, just as I had done since I was seven years old.

I jumped the last four feet onto the wet grass. That was a mistake. The hockey bag smacked me in the head when I landed. If this were a dream, how would I explain the big bump on my head when I woke up? I looked up to see if my dad was watching me from the window, and could have sworn I saw him waving me away. I began to run across the backyard with no idea where I was running. I vaulted over the landscaping bushes and kept running toward the trees behind our yard. It was really dark, and I had to be careful not to trip on any rocks.

I heard a strange noise behind me: a crackling sound and then a pop. I turned around. There was a strange light coming from my house. Then it happened: the loudest noise I ever heard. Two seconds later, I felt something hit me in the chest. I fell backward, my head hitting the ground. My ears began to ring, and I was dizzy. *Wow, look at all those stars.* I closed my eyes, but I could still see the stars.

When I reopened my eyes I saw tiny little lights everywhere. It smelled like something was burning. One of the lights floated down and touched my arm. It was hot, so I quickly brushed it off. I shook my head, but that made the ringing in my ears worse. My whole body felt weird. I could barely move my legs. There was another loud boom. I lifted my head to look at my house. Half of it was missing; the rest of it, on fire.

Oh my God, it must have blown up! "MOM! DAD!" I screamed at the top of my lungs. Over and over, I kept screaming. There was no answer. The night was silent again.

I was alone.

CHAPTER TWO

A big black Cadillac sat in the shadows, safely hidden from the view of any casual observer. Its driver, a big-nosed unpleasant-looking fellow with slicked-back hair, was enjoying the show. He counted the fire engines as they arrived.

"They're gonna need a lot more of them trucks," he said to the elegantly dressed man sitting in the backseat. "Ain't nothin' could survive that!"

"Tony, you talk too much!" the rear passenger stated.

While one fireman jumped off the pump truck with the input hose in search of the hydrant, another maneuvered the ladder truck into position. More sirens sounded in the distance.

Detective Tim Faraday pounded on the steering wheel while listening to the police dispatcher's voice. He picked up the mike and said, "Car 73 responding and out."

"Damn you, Jack, you've been working on this case for over six weeks," he yelled to the windshield. "I knew something like this was going to happen. You should have let me help you. You can't do everything yourself." He flipped on the siren and pushed the Crown Vic to the limit. As he approached the house, he could see the amber glow of the flames. The smell of burnt wood seeped through the car's windows.

Tony ducked low in the driver's seat when the police car passed. "What are we waitin' here for?" he asked. There was no answer from the back.

Tim Faraday jumped out of his cruiser and ran toward what was left of the burning house. Two firemen grabbed him. Tim flashed his badge. "I don't care who you are," one of them shouted. "It's not safe to go in there." Tim yanked his arm free and continued running. "Stop!" yelled the firemen in unison. It was no use. Tim had already entered the house.

"Look at that guy," Tony said. "That cop is crazier than you." For that remark, Tony felt the back of his seat get kicked.

"Jack, Carol, Adam, are you in here?" Tim screamed through the smoke. He could barely breathe, and it felt like his body was roasting. "Jack, Carol, Adam, answer me. Are you okay?" His loud screams carried to the street.

"Who the heck is Adam?" Tony asked.

"Jack's kid," the rear passenger replied.

"I didn't know that Jack had a kid," said Tony.

"You don't know about a lot of things," the passenger said.

"Well, I know one thing: ain't no one is survivin' that fire. When I'm told to make a problem disappear I know how to turn it to toast," Tony replied. "That's a guarantee!"

"Tony, there are no guarantees. You thought the Eagles were never going to win the Super Bowl. Anything can happen at any time. We just have to be prepared. If Jack's kid managed to survive, we must find him. He may know something, and we can't take any chances."

"How old is this kid, anyway?" Tony asked.

"I think around thirteen."

Tony laughed. "You're scared of a little kid? He don't even drive yet. Where's he gonna go?"

"That's what I want you to find out. And, Tony, don't screw this up. That thirteen-year-old kid might be smarter than you think. This is serious, Tony. No games. You find me that kid!"

"I got it, boss. If that kid is out there, I'll grab him."

Tony started the car and slowly drove away.

CHAPTER THREE

It was ten minutes past one in the morning. The Trent house stood in the darkness surrounded by a handful of 200-year-old maple trees, one of which loomed precariously close to Anthony's rear bedroom window. Adam had climbed that old tree hundreds of times, but never after one in the morning. Before he hoisted himself up on the first branch, Adam wiped the tears from his eyes. Cool kids should never cry, even if their house just blew up with their parents inside. It wasn't going to be easy to be cool in front of his friend Anthony.

He shimmied across the top branch and rapped on Anthony's window, not so hard as to wake up the whole family, but just enough to pull Anthony out of a dream. What Adam wasn't expecting was Anthony's dog, Ginger, to suddenly appear at the window. All Adam saw were two golden eyes and four huge white fangs. He almost fell off the tree. Recognizing Adam, the golden retriever wagged her tail so hard that the wind sent Anthony's model dinosaur crashing to the ground. Anthony was awake now, and possibly so was his entire family. He opened the window to let Adam in.

"Hey, man, how's it going?" Anthony asked. He looked at his glow-in-the-dark watch. "Don't you have anything better to do than scare me half to death at one in the morning?"

"First of all, your watch is slow; it's one fifteen. Second of all, this dog of yours almost gave me a heart attack," Adam replied as he tried to pull his hand out of Ginger's mouth. "What's up with Ginger? She won't stop licking me."

"She really likes you," Anthony replied.

"Yeah, well, I like her too, but you don't see me putting her paws in my mouth," Adam said while continuing to wrestle his hand from Ginger's tongue. "Jeez, doesn't this dog ever stop? Go eat something else!" he commanded the dog.

Anthony turned on his TV, which gave just enough light for him to see Adam's strange appearance. Anthony was not a member of the fashion police, but he couldn't help but offer his opinion about Adam's choice of evening wear.

"Nice duds. Who picked them out for you? Your father?"

Adam held his emotions in check. "Yeah, actually, he did. You got a problem with that?"

"No. That's cool. But what's up with the hockey bag? Did you join a midnight league or something?"

"Will you shut up for a minute and listen?" Adam asked. "There's something I have to tell you."

Adam told Anthony about how his father had woke him up, packed his clothes in the hockey bag, and pushed him out the window. Adam took a deep breath and described the weird noise, the force that knocked him down, the stars, the burning lights, and, finally, what happened to his house.

"Very funny," Anthony said. "And I guess you're going to tell me about the space aliens that are after you. Anything else happen tonight?"

"Yes," Adam replied. He was really trying to hold back the tears. "My parents were in the house when it blew up. They're dead!"

"And you expect me to believe this story of yours?" Anthony asked.

"It's the truth. I swear it! Why can't you believe it?"

"Well, for one thing, it's the craziest story I ever heard. Why would your father push you out the window? Who would blow up your house with your parents inside? And if your parents were dead, I think you would be crying your eyes out. You know, Adam, your mom may be the best drama teacher that our school has ever had, but I swear I never saw an actor as good as you. What does your mom do? Give you lessons at night or something?"

Maybe holding back the tears wasn't a good idea, Adam thought. "But I am telling you the truth. I swear it! Look at the TV."

Anthony couldn't believe what he saw. A news reporter was standing in front of Adam's smoldering house, talking about the explosion.

"It's true? You're not lying?" Anthony asked.

"No, I'm not lying," Adam replied. Then he remembered the piece of paper his father had shoved into his back pocket. He pulled it out. "Look, my dad gave me this!"

He unfolded the paper and began to read it.

Adam, I know you are very confused, but this letter will explain everything. First of all, you might be in great danger. Don't trust anybody. Things aren't what they seem. And don't go to your friend Anthony's house. They may look for you there, and it may place him in danger. What I want you to do is–

"Hey, check it out: they're talking about you on TV."

Adam placed the letter behind him on the bed and turned up the volume.

"Less than an hour ago, a house on a quiet street in Huntingdon Valley exploded. The fire marshal has not yet finalized his investigation, but he has determined that it was not due to a faulty gas line. He suggested that it might be a case of arson. What we do know is that all three occupants were home at the time. The fire marshal said the victims might not be found because of the intense heat of the fire. The names of the family members have just been released: police detective Jack Simmons; Huntingdon High's drama teacher, Carol Simmons; and their thirteen-year-old son, Adam."

"Hmm, now that I look at you, you are pretty handsome...for a dead kid!" Anthony laughed.

"Shut up!" Adam said while wiping the tears from his eyes. He reached back to get his father's letter. It was gone. "Okay, wise guy, where did you put the letter?"

"I never touched it!" Anthony replied.

"Then where is it?" Adam asked.

They looked over at Ginger, who was still chewing. By the time they got her mouth open, the letter was gone!

"I can't believe your dumb dog ate my dad's letter!" Adam shouted. "Now what am I supposed to do?"

"Didn't you read it?" Anthony asked.

"Not all of it, but just enough to know that I should never have come here."

"Why don't we check your hockey bag? Maybe your dad put something in there," Anthony said.

Before Adam could reply, Anthony had the bag unzipped and was rummaging through it. "Look what I found: a wallet!"

"Give me that!" Adam said and grabbed it from Anthony's hand. The wallet was the only thing left that had belonged to his father. Now it belonged to him. It was the most important thing he would ever own.

"What's your Gameboy doing in here? Cool. Do you mind if I borrow it?" Anthony asked.

"Sure. Whatever. Listen, I've got to go," Adam said.

"Where are you going?"

"I don't know yet. All I know is that I can't stay here. I'll be in touch." Adam grabbed the hockey bag and started out the window. "Yo, Anthony!"

"Yeah, Adam?"

"You didn't see me tonight—just in case anybody asks you."

"Sure, Adam. Whatever."

CHAPTER FOUR

Tony was in the car, sweeping the neighborhood. He figured that the kid, Adam, if he was alive (which was impossible), couldn't be more than a mile or two away. Searching for a kid was a total waste of Tony's talent.

He was a bit of a legend back in Detroit. There, he was known as "Tony the Match." He knew more about fire than the famous Dillon Liyans, Detroit's big fire commissioner. He used to play with Dillon's head all the time. He remembered the day he set six warehouses on fire, all across the city, at the same time. Each fire had been a five-alarmer. It had sounded like an air raid with all those sirens going at the same time. Every street had been clogged with cars trying to get out of the way of all those fire trucks. They had been coming and going in every direction. It had been sweet, real sweet.

Dillon Liyans had gone all over the place, from fire to fire, looking for evidence. Of course, Tony had made sure that nothing could be found. He was an expert. He was Tony the Match. All Dillon could say was that it had been the act of six separate arsonists. Now, that was a joke. Six arsonists, setting six fires, at the same time—sure, that could happen, and so could Christmas in July.

After eight years of fun and games, Tony had to leave Detroit. You might say it was getting a little "hot" for him there. Tony had to cool it for a while. He found that Philly was just the ticket. It wasn't a bad town to get lost in. He put the word on the streets that he was available;

no job too small. The local "guys" gave him a visit. Tony played dumb, which was easy with a huge, misshapen nose that had been broken on numerous occasions and a forehead that would've been better suited on a gorilla; playing dumb matched his looks. They quickly put the deal on the table. It wasn't a bad offer, not bad at all. Tony the Match became Tony the Wheel.

Driving the boss was a decent gig. When Tony got bored, the boss let him have a little fun. "Just don't burn the whole town down," the boss would say, and Tony would answer, "I ain't as dumb as I look!" The boss would always laugh at that one.

Huntingdon Valley gots some pretty nice digs, Tony thought as he drove up Bright Drive. *Man, check it out. That house over there belonged to the guy who used to own the 'Sixers. Not a bad basketball team, but ain't nothin' like they were back when they had Dr. J.*

He took out the night scope and turned on the switch. It was weird how the electronic glasses let you see in the dark. Everything appeared bright green. It took a little getting used to, but Tony had no problem at all. Night scoping was a favorite hobby of his. As he swept the hood, he noticed a lot of cats, but there was no kid in sight. He picked up his cell phone and made a call. "You got anything for me?" he asked one of his cohorts. Tony needed a little history on the kid. Sixty seconds later he had the car turned around. *And the boss thinks I got no brains,* he thought. *If I ain't got brains, then how come I know where the kid's best friend lives?*

He took a left on Hunting Pike and passed Bayberry Road in search of Fetter's Mill Lane. The old Bryn Athyn Cathedral was on the right; the sign said it was built in 1870. Legend had it that it was built for the queen of Sweden who set up a colony here called Bryn Athyn. All Tony knew was that it was one of the biggest churches he had ever seen.

The entrance to Fetter's Mill Lane was wedged between two giant cypress trees; their branches intertwined to form a misshapen arch over the driveway. The winding road led to a dilapidated railroad station, which was labeled the Bryn Athyn Post Office. At first, Tony thought he had reached a dead end, but then he saw that the road continued beyond the neglected railroad tracks. He crossed over a covered bridge that was barely wide enough for his car. To the left of the bridge was a hundred-year-old two-story stone building; a sign indicated that it was a historical landmark. *Yeah, maybe the queen of Sweden slept here,* he thought.

Three blocks past the historical building was Old Walsh Road, the street where Anthony Trent lived. He couldn't believe that kid could have gone this far on foot. "Nah, I'm wastin' my time. The kid is dead!"

He parked on a side street, took his night scope, and proceeded on foot without caring if he destroyed the freshly planted rows of flowers that were just beginning to bud.

He stood behind a tree at a fifty-foot distance and scoped the front area of the darkened house. Light-green ripples in a rectangular shape reflected from the right. It was a pool; they always cast that appearance through the scope. He could see nothing as he lifted his gaze, peering through the front windows. The shades were drawn to the very bottom of the sills.

Tony moved cautiously to the rear of the house. Standing behind another tree, he could make out a small, flickering light filtering through an upper bedroom window. *Somebody musta fallen asleep with the TV on,* he thought.

Suddenly, there was a noise, more like a thud, not a sound that any small animal would make. It came from a big tree near the window that had the flickering TV light. Tony worked his gaze from the top to the bottom of the tree. That was when he saw the bottom branch moving up and down slightly, as if someone had jumped off. He quickly scanned the grounds near the tree and saw a bright green image in the shape of a person. It was a boy wearing a large backpack.

"Yo, kid, what are you doin' back here?" Tony shouted with authority.

The boy turned, saw Tony, and bolted to the other side of the house.

"Wait, kid, I wanna talk to you!" Tony shouted and took off after the boy. He heard a garage door open around the corner.

"I gotcha now!" Tony exclaimed as he ran toward what appeared to be a shed. He was only twenty feet away when the boy left the shed on a bike, pedaling at top speed.

"Is your name Adam?" Tony shouted, out of breath, while running after the bike. The boy just gave Tony the finger as he sped away.

"I'm gonna get ya, kid! You ain't seen the last of me! I'll find ya no matter where you go!" Tony screamed.

CHAPTER FIVE

It was 2:30 a.m. On the second floor of the deserted police administration building, detective Tim Faraday sat at his desk searching for the paper on which he had scribbled some information no less than four hours earlier. As a second-year detective, he still hadn't learned the value of jotting things down in an electronic PDA. His argument was that if the tablet was hacked or if its battery went dead, it would be worthless. Today was different, though: he couldn't find what he needed. He knew he had it somewhere. It was a sheet from one of those yellow memo pads. There it was, under some manila folders: black scribbles of notes he had taken of his partner's last phone conversation.

An hour before the home blew up, Jack had called Tim explaining the case he had been working on. It was an incredible story about how his wife, Carol, had caught a boy doing drugs at Huntingdon High. Like most kids, the boy hadn't thought it was a big deal, but Carol had known the dangers of drugs. She was very convincing as she had explained how even "a little bit of illegal drugs" could quickly ruin someone's life. Eventually, the kid had revealed the drug dealer's name, and Jack had followed the drug trail to a Philly mob that apparently thought Huntingdon Valley would be a nice place to set up shop. Jack had mentioned that he'd gone undercover for the last six weeks. Tim had been about to warn Jack of the danger he might bring his family if he were caught, when something had gone wrong. Jack had mentioned something about Carol being—Tim remembered how the phone had gone dead before Jack finished what he had to say. The phone conversation with Jack ended as mysteriously and abruptly as it had begun.

Huntingdon Valley had only two police detectives. It was a small town with small problems. Kids did little things like vandalizing mailboxes or stealing tire valve caps. Drug use was pretty low on the totem pole. Apparently, even a town like Huntingdon Valley was not safe from the clutches of the mob. Being the only detective left on the force, Tim Faraday, a cop without a PDA, had to deal with the biggest crime puzzle the Huntingdon Valley Police Department had ever had. The first thing on his list was something he had thought he would not have to do for many years. In the next few days, he had to attend the funeral of Jack, Carol, and Adam Simmons. Until then, he would try to make sense of the worst tragedy this sleepy town had ever seen.

The fire marshal stated that it was an act of arson. If that was the case, then who did it? Logic pointed to the mob. Maybe they found out where Jack lived. Jack must have uncovered some evidence that had to be destroyed. But Jack had been a careful guy. If he had been undercover, he would have never led them to his house. There must have been a leak somewhere. Maybe someone else in the police department knew what Jack had been doing. And then there was the unfinished conversation about Carol. She was the one who had initiated this series of events. Could the mob have gotten to her?

Using his desk computer, Tim combed through the police data files for known arsonists. The Philly files didn't have much to go on, so he did a national search, and hundreds of names appeared on the screen. One in particular caught his attention—Tony the Match!

CHAPTER SIX

Adam had borrowed Anthony's bike many times in the past, but never at 2:30 in the morning. It was a ten-speed AMX mountain roadster with a heavy-duty dual-fork suspension, which was a good thing because Adam intended to go riding where no bike had gone before. After giving that crazy maniac the finger, he proceeded at top speed through the woods behind Anthony's house. Anthony had told him about how he used to walk through the woods to his grandfather's house. Adam hoped that he hadn't been lying, because where he was headed was not too far from where Anthony's grandfather lived.

Speeding in the dark was treacherous. Between the rocks, holes, and tree roots, Adam swore that he'd never attempt riding in the woods by the light of the moon again. After dumping the bike four times and scraping both knees and an elbow, he finally emerged through a small clearing behind Grandpa Trent's house.

He walked the bike cautiously around the perimeter of the house, being careful not to activate the outside motion detector lights. The last thing he needed was to wake Grandpa Trent. Grandpa had a gun collection and would think nothing about shooting a prowler. When he reached the front garage he remounted the bike and coasted down the long driveway to the street.

He made a left turn on Fetter's Mill Lane and continued on the winding road until reaching the covered bridge. He smiled as the old stone building came into sight. He and Anthony had once deemed it their clubhouse; that was until they were chased away by a guy who worked at the Bryn Athyn post office. He wouldn't have to worry about that until the morning. For now it was the perfect place to hide. He needed a place to think things out, a place to sleep. His only concern was bumping into the queen of Sweden's ghost!

He climbed through a small window in the back of the building. After unlatching the interior lock of the rear door, he opened it and pulled the bike inside.

The smell of mold and mildew combined with the stench of Adam's sweat permeated the dark recesses of the 200-hundred-year-old basement. Adam shivered in the dampness. The old clubhouse appeared quite different at this ungodly hour.

He climbed the stone staircase to the upper level. There was some light provided by the five-watt electric candles that were mounted on the sill of each window. The candles in the windows always gave an inviting look from the street when you drove by at night. This was the first time Adam saw the candles from the inside looking out.

He sat for a while, staring out the window, wondering what to do next. He soon spotted a car's headlights coming in his direction. Trying not to burn his fingers on the hot bulb, he carefully unscrewed the bulb just enough for the light to go out. He crouched slightly and moved behind one of the old wooden shutters. As the headlights grew closer, he was nearly invisible to anyone looking up at the window.

His heart raced as the car slowed down in front of the building. Holding his breath, he began to pray. He could make out the silhouette of the driver. It was too dark to see any details, but what he could see scared the daylights out of him! Bright green lights were shooting out of the driver's eyes, and they were staring right at him. It seemed like forever before the car started moving again. Adam, now red in the face due to a lack of oxygen, began to breathe a sigh of relief. He watched the car continue over the covered bridge, stopping a few more times in search of something. Evidently, the green-eyed monster was curious about the stream that ran under the bridge. The car turned into the post office parking lot and sat for a while. The whole time as he watched, Adam could see the bright green lights scanning back and forth. Adam's fear factor rose as the green-eyed alien who drove a black Cadillac left the car and carefully walked to the back of the post office. And then God must have heard Adam's prayers. The driver from outer space finally got into the car and drove away.

This was all too much for a thirteen-year-old to handle. His parents were dead. His house and all of his belongings had been blown to bits. The important note his father had given him was gone because of a stupid dog's appetite. A crazy man was chasing after him. And now to top everything off: green-eyed space aliens! Worst of all, he might have placed his best friend in danger.

He was tired and totally alone with no place to go. Adam didn't want to be cool any longer.

He cried.

CHAPTER SEVEN

Tony couldn't believe that he had missed grabbing the kid as he rode by on the bike. But what bothered him more was that the kid's name might have been Adam. He kept thinking that there was no way Adam could have survived the fire, but who else could it have been? If it were just some neighborhood boy, what was he doing out so late at night? And why was he running away? The biggest clue was when the kid had given him the finger when Tony had asked for his name.

The kid must have more lives than a cat! Tony thought. He knew a great deal about cats since he'd had three growing up. They could be tricked.

After seeing the boy ride into the woods, Tony ran back to his car, hoping to catch him when he emerged from the other side. He spun the car around, headed back on Old Walsh Road, and made a left onto Fetter's Mill Lane. Driving slowly with his right hand, he used his night scope to sweep the woods with his left. He looked for bike tire marks under the bridge, but there wasn't a trace of a tread. He even searched behind the post office for footprints. The kid was nowhere to be found. He had just vanished into thin air.

He thought about going back to Anthony's house but scratched the idea for the time being. Instead, he made a phone call. The boss was not pleased about a 3:30 a.m. phone conversation. Tony tried to explain the situation, but the boss wouldn't hear it. "If you can't do the job, then I'll find somebody else!" he kept screaming.

Tony was too tired to argue. Besides, arguing with the boss could get you killed. He wasn't even sure that the kid he was chasing was really Adam. Deciding to go back to Anthony's house might not be such a bad idea. He would wait there and grab some shut-eye until the sun rose. Then he would make his move.

At 7:15 a.m. Anthony stood outside his house waiting for the school bus to arrive. He was fifteen minutes early—just enough time to play with Adam's Gameboy. The problem was that it wouldn't work. He was shoving it back into his schoolbag when a tall man wearing a long black coat approached him.

"Morning, kid," the man said.

Anthony responded with a nod of his head.

"I'm with the Huntingdon Valley police," said the man while showing Anthony the bright, shiny badge that he had retrieved from his inside coat pocket.

"What's up?" Anthony asked.

The policeman pointed to Anthony's garage shed and answered, "That door is."

"Yeah, so what?" Anthony replied.

"There have been some robberies in the area," the policeman pointed out. "I'm supposed to check 'em out. That garage door might have been left open all night. Maybe we should look to see if anything coulda been stolen."

Reluctantly, Anthony followed the man to the garage.

"Anything gone?" the officer asked.

Anthony took a quick inventory. Everything was there except his AMX bike. He realized that Adam must have taken it.

"Nope. Nothing missing," he answered nervously.

"You know, after the fire last night, everybody is a little nervous," the officer said.

Anthony played dumb. "What fire?" he asked.

"The fire that burnt down the Simmons' house," he replied. "It was a big one. A cop, a teacher, and a thirteen-year-old boy died in that fire. Maybe you knew the kid. I think his name was Adam."

"Yeah, I know him. We are good friends," Anthony said.

"No kiddin'," the man replied. "You don't look too upset about his death."

Anthony had an attack of nervousness again. "Yeah, well, I am upset. I just don't show it much."

"You must be a real cool kid to hide your feelings that good," complimented the man.

"Thanks," Anthony replied. "Listen, I have to go. I'm going to miss my bus."

"Sure, kid. No problem," the man returned. "I'll walk you to the bus stop by your house. My car is just across the street."

"Sure, whatever," Anthony replied.

"By the way, kid, when you saw Adam last night, did he happen to give you anything?"

"No!" Anthony answered.

"Was that: No, he didn't give you anything, or no, you didn't see him?" asked the man.

Anthony thought for a moment and nervously replied, "What makes you think I saw Adam last night?"

The bus engine could be heard as it rounded the corner. Anthony looked over and pointed to the man's car.

"That's your car?" he asked.

"Yeah, it's a nice one," the man answered. "The Chevy Caprice they gave me at the station wouldn't start, so I took this one instead."

Anthony knew about cars. For one thing, only the police in Philly drove Caprices. The police around here drove Ford Crown Victorias. He watched as the man across the street got into a black Cadillac and drove away.

Chapter Eight

Tim Faraday was tired and hungry. The last time he had pulled an all-nighter was in college. His eyes were bleary from staring at the Dell fifteen-inch flat-screen monitor touted as having the best resolution. The only resolution Tim cared about was solving this nightmare of a case and going to bed. The information he had gathered so far was minimal at best. Most of it was based on coincidence and supposition. He wished he could call Jack for his opinion, but that was impossible. Instead, he closed his eyes and prayed to the spirit of Jack for inspiration.

The mere fact that Tony the Match had left Chicago and was now in Philly didn't necessarily mean that he was responsible for the burning of Jack's house. Rumor had it that Tony was now driving for the mob. All Tim had to do was prove that Tony the Match was in Huntingdon Valley the night of the fire. That would be enough to pull him in for questioning. Of course, a guy like Tony would probably not admit to anything under interrogation. But that was okay. Sometimes it's what you don't say that counts.

Tim was reluctant to follow the directions in the police detective's handbook. It was routine that friends and relatives of the victims be questioned whenever there was a homicide. He knew that it was probably a waste of time, but it had to be done. He grabbed a few blank sheets of paper from the clutter on his desk and headed downstairs.

It was 8:00 a.m. and there was an indication of life at the station. The smell of freshly brewed coffee was in the air. A box of Dunkin' donuts lay half open at the complaint desk. He wondered if anyone would complain when they found a jelly-filled missing. His lips were covered with white powdered sugar when he proceeded out the back door to the parking lot.

A coating of black soot dulled the white hood of his Crown Vic. His first stop would not be related to the investigation.

The American Car Wash was located about two miles north of the police station. Although it was in the opposite direction of Anthony's house, Tim thought it best to wash the car before he visited the Trents. He remembered how Jack used to lecture him about keeping the car clean at all times. Jack would say that people often judge you by the way your car looks. A clean car indicates good organization and attention to details. Tim figured it was easier to keep the car clean than to learn how to work a PDA tablet.

By 9:00 a.m. a shiny Crown Victoria stood under the oak tree in front of the Trent home. Tim exited the car and looked up at the hummingbird that was perched on an upper branch, making a melodic racket.

"Don't even think about messing on my car," he warned the winged singer.

He could hear the splat on the car's hood just as he reached the steps of the house.

"Good morning. Mrs. Trent, right?" he asked, when the slim woman answered the door. Although she and Tim had never formally met, she fit Jack's description perfectly. Tim and Jack used to play the description game. Jack would describe someone, and Tim would have to pick the person out of a crowd. Phyllis Trent was a good-looking woman who looked years younger than any woman with a thirteen-year-old. Her blonde shoulder-length hair was tied in a cute ponytail. She had a hurried look about her. Tim hoped he wasn't disturbing her.

"Yes, I'm Phyllis Trent. What can I do for you, Officer?" Her voice sounded slightly perturbed. "I don't mind helping the police, but I have places to go this morning."

"Mrs. Trent, this will only take a minute."

"That's what the other detective said, but it was certainly longer than a minute!" she snapped.

Tim Faraday was very confused, and it must have shown on his face.

"Look, I'm sorry if I appear rude, but that other detective was a bit pushy. I'm not used to being talked to in an abusive manner. You can catch more flies with honey, you know!" she continued.

"Yes, ma'am," Tim replied, still bewildered.

"And don't call me ma'am! You make it sound like I'm old!" She opened the door wider. "Please come in. I didn't catch your name."

"Detective Tim Faraday," he responded with an outstretched hand.

She shook it gently and said, "Please, call me Phyllis."

"Okay, Phyllis it is. I must tell you, I'm somewhat confused. You say that there was another detective?"

"Yes. He showed me his badge and said that he was following up on some kind of drug problem at Huntingdon High. I explained that my son, Anthony, doesn't attend the high school. He's still at Morry Avenue Middle School."

"What did he do then, Mrs. Trent?"

"Please don't call me Mrs. Trent. It sounds like you're talking to my mother-in-law!"

"No problem. What did he do when you told him that your son doesn't attend Huntingdon High, Phyllis?"

"He asked if he could look at Anthony's room. Anthony is no angel, but I know he's too smart to do drugs! I let the detective look at his room."

"Did he take anything?" Tim Faraday asked.

"No. He just opened a few drawers and poked around a bit. Then he told me he had other things to do and left," Phyllis explained.

"When exactly did this take place?" Tim asked.

"About an hour ago," Phyllis stated.

"This morning?" Tim asked.

"Of course, this morning! Isn't that why you are here?"

"No, ma'am—I mean Phyllis. I'm here to talk about last night's fire at the Simmons' residence."

"There was a fire at Adam Simmons's house? Was anyone hurt?" she asked.

Tim hated this part of his job. "Yes, ma'am, I'm afraid there was."

"Who? Who got hurt?" she asked.

"The whole family," he managed to gulp out.

"Are they okay?" she asked.

Tim Faraday attempted to swallow the lump in his throat before trying to answer. "No, ma'am, they're dead."

"Oh my Lord," Phyllis uttered. She placed her hands over her face and began to cry. "Adam was Anthony's best friend," she sobbed, "and Gina, as well! The three of them would spend hours together doing homework projects."

"Yes, ma'am, I understand. Could you describe the officer who visited you?"

"He was tall and... I just can't believe that they're dead!"

"No, ma'am, neither can I." He could see that she was too distraught. "I'll come back another time, ma'am."

She looked up with tear-stained eyes and said, "Phyllis—not ma'am!"

"Yes, ma'am—I mean Phyllis," Tim responded and left.

CHAPTER NINE

Normally, the solid oak door was left open, but this day, not only was it closed, it was locked. Tony took a deep breath and knocked three times. Hearing no response, he rapped on the door seven more times with all his strength.

"Isn't that door locked?" a voice bellowed from the other side.

"Yeah, boss, it is," Tony replied.

"Do you know why it's locked?" asked the voice.

"Because you don't want nobody bothering you?" Tony guessed.

"Exactly! Let me see, who do I know that would bother me today? Would that be Tony?"

"Yeah, boss, it's me." Tony hated the way the boss put him down. "It's important!"

"Oh, it's important. Well, that's a relief. I thought you were going to bother me with something stupid! In that case, maybe I should unlock the door before you knock another ten times and break it down."

There was a click and the door opened.

"Thanks, boss," Tony said through clenched teeth.

"Tony, I want to introduce you to Mr. Irving."

A medium-sized gray-haired older man with an oversized equally gray mustache stood up from the table. He wore a white shirt with an old bow tie at the collar. Over the shirt was a plaid cardigan sweater. When he extended his hand, Tony noticed that the man's grip was very weak.

"Mr. Irving is doing some accounting for me," the boss announced. "He came highly recommended and used to do some work for Big Phil Lieb's gang in Jersey."

Tony nodded his head even though he'd never heard of Big Phil Lieb or his gang. "Yeah, well, boss, what I gotta say should be in private."

The boss laughed. He pointed to the hearing aids in Mr. Irving's ears. "I seriously doubt that Mr. Irving cares about what you have to say. Besides, if you talk softly enough, he won't even be able to hear you. You do know how to talk softly, don't you?"

Tony took a deep breath to help hold in his anger. "Sure, boss," he answered softly.

"Well, what is this important bit of information you have?" asked the boss.

Tony looked at Mr. Irving, who appeared to be studying some papers. He seemed totally disinterested in what Tony had to say.

"It's about the kid," Tony began. "I did some checking, and I think he really is alive."

The boss's eyebrows lifted. "I told you that last night, didn't I? Have you found him yet?"

"Not yet, boss, but I know where he's been. He's got this friend, Anthony, who he visited last night. I questioned the kid."

"You questioned the boy?"

"Yeah, boss. I showed him a badge and told him I was a cop. Then I searched his room."

"He let you search his room?"

"Nope, I used my head and waited for him to go to school. Then I visited his mother. She ain't a bad looker. Anyways, she bought my cop story and let me have a go at the kid's room. She thought I was looking for drugs. I looked real good. She was pretty happy when I found no drugs. The fact is that I found nothing, boss. I don't think that kid, Adam, gave his friend nothing."

"So where is Adam now?" the boss asked.

"Like I told you, I'm still working on that."

"Tony, let me make it so clear that even a person of your intelligence can understand. I want Adam NOW! I don't want stories of how he eludes you. Now, if this job is too hard for you, then maybe I should give it to someone more qualified, like Mr. Irving over there."

Mr. Irving lifted his head up slightly and smiled.

Tony looked at Mr. Irving and snarled, "That ain't necessary, boss."

Mr. Irving stood as Tony was about to leave. He extended his hand once more in friendship. Reluctantly, Tony shook it again, squeezing it even harder this time. To his surprise, Mr. Irving squeezed back with a grip of iron.

The boss relocked the door after Tony's exit. He silently contemplated his next move.

"It looks like you have a small problem on your hands," Mr. Irving stated.

The boss looked somewhat surprised. "I thought you had a hearing problem?"

"Some days my ears work a little better than others. Today must be one of those days."

Mr. Irving thumbed through some of the papers he was working on. "By my calculations, it appears that, over the last month or so, your business is on the right track. You have a forty-percent increase over last year's profit of $3 million—and that would be after-tax profit."

The boss laughed and said, "Taxes? Since when should the government share in my drug profits? Should I fill out a tax form and tell them what I do for a living?"

"No, of course not," Mr. Irving replied, "but, as a public accountant, I must advise you of the consequences of your actions."

"You stick to advising me on how rich I am becoming. I only have one concern at the moment, and unfortunately I have an idiot taking care of that matter!"

"Perhaps I could assist you in that endeavor?" Mr. Irving asked.

"You? Ha! You're an old man. I just mentioned using you to make Tony angry. You didn't think I was serious, did you?"

"Please forgive me, sir. I work with percentages every day. In my opinion, two people looking for the boy may increase the chances of finding him."

A slow smile crept across the boss's face. "When I hired you a few weeks ago I had my doubts, but now I can see that you are a real asset to my organization. I think I am going to take your advice. Two people will certainly find the boy faster."

"May I make another suggestion, sir?" Mr. Irving asked.

"Is this about paying my taxes?" the boss replied.

"No, sir. It appears that you have no intention of doing that. It's about finding the boy, Adam."

"Don't tell me you know where he is?" the boss asked.

"Not at the moment. But I think I know where he is going," Mr. Irving replied.

"And just where might that be?"

"Why, the funeral, of course!" Mr. Irving stated quite adamantly.

"The funeral?" the boss asked.

"That's correct. It stands to reason that Adam wouldn't miss his parents' funeral. I take it that they will be holding a funeral for him as well. And then there's the matter of the eulogy. It's not often that a child gets to hear how people truly feel about him." Mr. Irving smiled as he said each word slowly and distinctly.

The boss nodded his head in approval. "Mr. Irving, you are a pleasant surprise."

"I'm glad you feel that way. Yes, you'll find that I can be full of surprises."

CHAPTER TEN

An intricate pattern appeared on the wall as the sun streamed its light through the cobwebs that had been spun across the window. It was slightly past 1:00 p.m., and the parking lot across the street was filled with cars making their momentary stops. Adam wiped the residue of sleep from the corners of his eyes and carefully peered out the window. The train station post office looked quite different at this time of day. Slowly, the memories of the previous night returned. Nothing made sense—especially the green-eyed alien. He pushed the tears and sadness of his parents' death back as far as he could so they wouldn't interfere with what he had to do.

He needed a disguise. The man chasing him could recognize him, and everyone else (except for Anthony) thought he was dead. He required a change of wardrobe, something to make him look older. Perhaps a mustache or a beard would help. It only took a minute or so to formulate the next move. He knew exactly where to find everything he needed.

Adam carefully managed his way down the hazardous stone steps to the lower level of the old historic building. Anthony's bike was right where he'd left it, leaning next to the rear door. He unbolted the door, rolled out the bike, and refastened the makeshift lock. Aside from the queen of Sweden's ghost, the building was just as vacant as it had been for the last hundred or so years.

Careful not to draw any attention from a postal employee or

customer, Adam maneuvered the bike under the bridge and continued on a small path at the water's edge. He dragged some branches on the moist ground behind him to mask the trail left by his footprints and the bike's tires. Happy with the results, he continued his trek until it was safe to climb back up on the road. He used some leaves to clean the mud from the tires before jumping on to continue his journey. Realizing that a passing car might spot him as he pedaled, he decided to take a shortcut through the woods. After ten minutes of biking uphill through tree roots, branches, and stones, his legs muscles were aching as he finally reached his destination: the Bryn Athyn Museum.

"The Bryn Athyn Museum was built in the early 1900s by Raymond Pit," Adam remembered the tour guide saying when his class took the tour last year. It was really a neat place. Mr. Pit had built it so he would have a place to put his collection of medieval objects. The church-like building was filled with galleries that displayed religious artifacts from the Israelites, Egyptians, Greeks, and Romans. There were even religious items from China and Native American Indians. With a little luck, Adam would have no problem finding the materials he needed for his disguise.

At the rear of the museum, Adam found some tattered brown tarps covering a rusted tractor. After hiding the bike under the tarps, he searched for an open window or door, but his high hopes were soon dashed as he discovered that everything was locked tighter than a drum. He would have to chance entering through the front lobby. Hopefully, there would be no tours in progress.

He traversed the stone pathway until he reached the front of the building. Hesitant to use the large brass door knockers, which were mounted at shoulder height on two huge arched wooden doors, he tried turning one of the old door knobs. To his surprise, he found that the doors were unlocked, so he pushed one of the doors open slightly and squeezed in. The lobby was just as colorful as he remembered it. Splashes of red, green, blue, and yellow lit the room as the sun played through the upper stained-glass windows. The marble floor was spotless, too clean to have been trampled on by a recent tour.

"Hello?" Adam said weakly, hoping for no response. *Maybe everyone is at lunch,* he thought. He quickly located the fire stairway and descended two flights to the basement, hoping to find a maintenance room or some such place where the building's blueprints were stored. As Adam searched the dimly lit basement hall, he heard what sounded like tapping behind him. Quickly spinning around, he saw nothing, but he continued his search with caution. The elusive tapping continued behind him. Though scared, a funny thought occurred to him: maybe the green-eyed alien had turned into an invisible tap dancer.

Determined to discover the source of the tapping, Adam turned the corner and hid behind a door. The tapping grew louder as it reached the end of the hall. Adam held his breath as the tapping neared the corner. Although he possessed no weapon, he could scream loud enough to give anybody a heart attack. If that didn't work, there was always the swift-kick-in-the-crotch plan.

Adam saw a shadow slowly creep across the hallway floor. It was like something he had never seen before. It was in the shape of an animal, but not like any animal that resided on planet Earth. The shadow showed a leg that ended in a point, and a head attached to a bowl-like neck. Hiding behind a door was no longer a good idea. Reluctantly, Adam decided to make a run for it. He jumped from behind the door, looked at the strange pursuer, and screamed.

"Who's there?" bellowed a voice from the far end of the darkened hall.

Adam could hardly breathe, and his heart was racing a mile a minute. What he saw startled him so that he broke out into uncontrollable laughter. Before him was the tap-dancing monster, a cute little French poodle. Its black furry right leg was wrapped in a bandage, and around its neck was a large plastic Victorian collar. Evidently, the collar was used to keep the dog from chewing off the bandage.

"Is anyone there?" yelled the distant voice.

Adam looked at the dog, put his index finger on his lips, and said, "Shhh!"

CHAPTER ELEVEN

Being angry, tired, and hungry did not improve Tony's disposition. He rummaged through the Cadillac's glove compartment searching for a candy bar. Finding a crumpled half of a Hershey bar, he stripped off its brown wrapper and popped it into his mouth. After satisfying his hunger for only the moment, he started the car and drove up Hunting Pike in search of a restaurant, preferably Italian.

Three miles north, on the left side of the street, was a sign that called to him: Aldo's Italian Café. Below the sign was a moderate-size brick building with four large arched windows spanning the front. Each window displayed colorful neon lights spelling out the specialties of the house: pizza, calzone, stromboli, lasagna. Tony couldn't pull the Cadillac into the parking lot fast enough.

Aldo's interior was a blend of Italian and American décor. The center of the dining room consisted of a romantic gallery of small, round wooden tables and chairs. Red checkerboard tablecloths adorned the tables. In the center of each table was a candle-dripped Chianti bottle. The perimeter of the room exhibited large green booths for family seating. The table at each booth had a vase of wild flowers and a bottle of mineral water. Tony felt right at home.

A cute girl danced her way to the table with a menu.

"Hi! My name is Ashley. Can I get you a drink?"

Tony smiled. A drink was just what he needed. "You got scotch?"

Ashley frowned. "No, just soda, but if you don't tell anyone, I might be able to get you some of Aldo's homemade wine."

Tony's eyebrows lifted. He remembered when his father had given him homemade wine direct from Italy. *"It has a real kick to it,"* his father had told him, *"probably because they squash the grapes with their feet."* Tony thought that was pretty funny. He looked at Ashley and asked, "Does Aldo have clean feet?"

Ashley was bemused. "I have no idea, but he has nice shoes," she confessed.

Tony laughed. "Bring on the vino, and a menu, too!" He watched as Ashley scurried away through a set of double swinging doors.

The wine and menu were wonderful. All the food descriptions made Tony's mouth water. He couldn't decide between the homemade meatballs or the calzone.

"I'll take the meatballs," he said. As Ashley retired to the kitchen, he shouted, "And a calzone on the side!"

Fifteen minutes later, Ashley returned with food fit for a king. The smell alone was enough to make you think that you had died and gone to heaven. Tony quickly grabbed his fork. With each taste came a moan of satisfaction. It was the best Italian food he had eaten since he was a child. The chef behind those swinging doors must have been a clone of his mother.

"Did Aldo make this?" he asked Ashley.

"Is there something wrong?" she asked.

"Ain't nothing wrong," he said while shoving another meatball into his mouth. "His cooking ain't bad. I just want to tell him, one Italian to another, that's all."

Ashley disappeared through the doors once again. A few minutes later a rather small Chinese man appeared at Tony's table.

"I ain't done yet!" Tony said.

"I can see that," the Chinese man replied.

"Yo, bud, you're blockin' my light! You can clean the table when I'm done. In the meanwhile, why don't you go clean a bathroom or somethin'?"

THE CHASE • 39

"Our bathrooms have been cleaned already. I was told that you wanted to see me?"

"That girl musta got it wrong. I asked to see Aldo!" Tony replied.

"I'm Aldo!" the Chinese man beamed with pride, "Aldo Siclione!"

"You can't be Aldo," Tony stated.

"And why is that?"

"Because you're Chinese!"

"I am?"

"Yeah, you are! Ain't you ever looked in a mirror?"

Aldo ran to the bathroom and took a peek. "Oh my God—*I'm Chinese*! he screamed. "I'll have to throw out all the spaghetti and start making lo mein!"

Tony was laughing when Aldo returned. "Yo, Aldo, you're a pretty funny guy."

"You should see me when I dress up as a geisha," Aldo replied. "Can I get you some dessert; a fortune cookie, perhaps?"

Tony pounded his fist on the table. "A fortune cookie and some bad green tea—now that's funny!"

Aldo was not amused.

"Lemme ask you somethin'. Where'd you learn to cook like this?"

Aldo bowed his head and said, "Old family recipe."

Tony chuckled. "Well, I ain't had food like this since I was a little boy. My mom, she was a good cook!"

"Was she Chinese?" Aldo asked.

"No," Tony replied.

"That's a shame," Aldo replied.

"I should tell all my friends about this place," Tony said.

"You have friends?" Aldo asked.

Now Tony was not amused. "That ain't funny!"

"I guess I'm a better chef than I am a comedian," Aldo replied.

"I like you," Tony said. "You're okay in my book!"

"What book is that? *Ancient Chinese Secrets*?" Aldo asked.

Tony laughed so hard that little pieces of meatballs fell onto his lap.

"Confucius say that man who eat meatball without napkin wear red pants!" Aldo stated.

Tony started pounding the table. He was laughing and gasping at the same time. "You're killin' me!" he managed.

Aldo quoted another proverb: "Man who die of laughter is happy to the end!"

CHAPTER TWELVE

Mr. Irving had assured the boss that he would find Adam before Tony did. He was hoping that he would have the boy within his grasp before the funeral. To a thirteen-year-old on a bicycle, Huntingdon Valley was a small town. Mr. Irving imagined himself as a young boy and envisioned all the places that someone like Adam would find desirable. Out of all the possibilities, the Bryn Athyn Museum had the most potential. The multitude of galleries would offer a wide variety of hiding locations. He would start in the basement and vigilantly search every level until the boy was found.

Mr. Irving was in the middle of probing the museum's boiler room when he heard what he thought was a scream coming from the far end of the basement hall. "Who's there?" he called out, but the only response he received was laughter. It was difficult to determine if the laughter was from a boy. He ran out into the hall, but it was too dark to see anything. Mr. Irving wanted to call out Adam's name but realized that it might further scare the boy. He had to make Adam come to him.

He noticed a dog bowl in the boiler room, which indicated that the maintenance man must have a four-legged companion. If he posed as the maintenance man looking for his dog, he would be less threatening to the boy. Judging from the size of the bowl, he guessed the dog to be small. He picked a name most fitting a small canine and called out, "Here, Tootsie. Tootsie, where are you? Do you want a treat?"

A weak bark emanated from the hall's end. Mr. Irving couldn't believe his luck. Either Tootsie was the dog's name, or it recognized the word *treat*. It was apparent that his plan was a spark of genius. He walked down the hall continuing to call out to the dog and bribing it with treats. The barking became louder as Mr. Irving approached.

"I have him!" he heard from the distance. It was definitely a boy's voice, the voice of Adam.

"Please hold little Tootsie for me," Mr. Irving replied. "I'm an old man. I can only walk so fast." He took off his shoes and started running down the hall as softly as he could. The barking grew louder and louder. Within a minute he would be there. The barking was coming from a room. All he had to do was open the door and grab the boy. "Gotcha!" he yelled as he quickly yanked the door open and turned on the light. The dog was there—but no boy. Sitting on the floor was a scrap of paper with a chain lying across the top. Mr. Irving picked up the paper.

It read, "I don't know who you are, but by the way you run, you're pretty fast for an old guy. I do know one thing, though: this dog doesn't belong to you!"

Mr. Irving looked at the chain. On it hung a small dog tag. He smiled as he read the tiny letters: Fifi. He realized how smart Adam was.

CHAPTER THIRTEEN

The highly publicized Simmons funeral had the largest attendance that Gold's Funeral Home had ever accommodated. The entire police department was in force to honor Detective Jack Simmons. Students and teachers representing both Huntingdon High and Morry Middle School were in attendance to pay their respects to their beloved drama teacher, Carol Simmons, and wonderful friend Adam Simmons. The chapel's normal seating capacity of 200 was extended by the addition of chairs that were placed in the side and back aisles. Even with all those extra seats, hundreds of people were left standing in the reception area and the outside parking lot. With the multitude of people came twice the amount of tears. Women and girls clutched tissues for comfort. Men and boys blotted their eyes with the backs of their hands.

Gina Nano had arrived an hour early hoping to get a front seat. Apparently, she wasn't the only person with that idea. Gina settled for a seat in the rear of the chapel. She was one of Adam's "chick" friends and had red eyes, the result of days of crying. She and Adam had teased each other incessantly through the ten years of their friendship. She had hated it when he had referred to her as Gina Nana Banana. Now, the very thought of it brought tears to her eyes. She found herself sitting between Anthony, who was on her right, dressed in a blue button-down shirt, and a young man with a mustache, dark sunglasses, a baseball cap, and a brightly colored t-shirt on her left.

At the front of the chapel were three caskets, a smaller silver rectangular box wedged between two larger ones, each with a bouquet of flowers eloquently placed on the top. No one questioned whether the coffins were symbolic or if they truly contained any remains of the bodies. The funeral director thought it best to wait until the room quieted down to proceed. Over an hour passed before he stepped to the podium.

"Friends, family, and relatives, on this sad occasion we come to pay our respects to three wonderful people, Jack, Carol, and Adam Simmons, who died in a tragic fire just a few short days ago."

From the front to the back of the chapel, an emotional wave of sadness moved through the sea of family and friends. The funeral director paused for a moment to allow the loudest sobbing to subside.

"In the history of Gold's Funeral Home, I cannot remember a single instance when we had a memorial for an entire family. It is so comforting that, as I stand before you, I see so many of you in attendance to honor the deceased. With great difficulty, I have decided to first eulogize the youngest of the Simmons family, Adam, who was an intelligent lad with looks that could charm anyone, especially some of the young ladies that I see before me."

At that moment, Gina's sobbing was so loud that Anthony had to whisper in her ear, "Gina, don't cry. Adam is okay."

"I know. He's in heaven now," she responded and continued her crying.

The young man on her left started to chuckle.

Gina turned to him and said, "How could you possibly see the humor in this?"

Before he could respond, she hit him in the side with her elbow.

"Adam had great potential," the director continued, "with his wonderful personality and tremendous communication skills; he had the potential to become a great statesman, quite possibly the President of the United States."

Now Anthony started to chuckle.

Gina turned to him, seething in anger, and said, "He would have made a *great* president!"

The young man on her left could barely hold his laugher. Gina used both her elbows to put a dent in the sides of each person. The young man on her left used his elbow to return the jab.

"I'm sure," said the director, "in our own way, Adam has touched each and every one of us. What would we say to him if he were here today?"

Gina found herself whispering, "I'd tell him that I loved him."

"What was that?" the young man on the left asked.

"Mind your own business!" Gina replied.

"Did you say you loved him?"

"Yes! That's what I said."

He smiled and said, "I love you!"

She elbowed him again. "You're a sicko! I don't even know you. How could you say such a thing at Adam's funeral?"

Anthony leaned over and said with a smile on his face, "Quiet down, you two. I can barely hear all the wonderful things being said about our next president."

Gina walloped them again with her elbows.

"It is so sad when we lose someone so dear," the director said. "If only we could turn the clock so we could again be with a loved one and share wonderful experiences."

The young man on the left held his side and said to Gina, "Please. No more experiences!"

"What are you talking about?" Gina asked.

"I can't take any more experiences," he replied.

"The director is talking about Adam, stupid, not you!" Gina pointed out.

"How can you call the person you love stupid?"

Gina was infuriated. She was about to hit him again when he quietly whispered, "I'm Adam."

She elbowed him as hard as she could, right between the ribs.

"You're killing me!" he gasped.

"If you were Adam, you couldn't possibly feel it, because you're dead!" She reached down to retrieve another tissue from her pocketbook. "And, you," she said to Anthony, "you were his best friend, and all you can do is laugh. If Adam was alive, he would hit you!"

"No, I wouldn't," the young man on the left said.

"I wasn't talking to you!" Gina hissed.

"No, she wasn't talking *to* you," Anthony added, "she was talking *about* you!"

"Now what are *you* talking about?" Gina asked Anthony.

"He's trying to tell you that I'm Adam, Gina Nana Banana!"

"What? What did you say?" she asked.

"I told you that I am Adam," he said.

"No. I meant after that."

"Oh. I called you Gina Nana Banana!"

She rammed her elbow with all her strength into his side, causing him to double over in pain.

"Don't you ever call me that! Adam was the only person who called me by that name."

The boy grimaced as he pushed back the pain. "That's exactly my point! And if you don't stop hitting me, I'll never talk to you again." He used one hand to lift his mustache and the other to lift his sunglasses.

"ADAM!" she screamed.

He quickly fixed his disguise. "Shhh. It's a secret! Everyone here thinks I'm dead!"

Hundreds of people turned their heads to see what the commotion was about. Gina had to think of something quickly.

"*Adam,* my dear Adam, I just can't go on without you!" she screamed and then fainted.

"She needs some air," the two boys said in unison. They both stood and pulled Gina to her feet. Gina had let her body go limp, making it very difficult for the boys to lift her. With Anthony's help, Adam managed to get her on his shoulder.

"I can't believe how much she loved him," he said loudly. It looked like he was having trouble carrying her. What everyone didn't know was that Gina was pinching him the entire way to the exit.

"Cut it out," he whispered to her.

"You say one more stupid thing about how much I loved you and you will wish you *were* dead," she whispered back.

As they made their way to the back door, Anthony had noticed someone familiar.

"See that guy over there? He was at my house the other day asking me questions. He said he was a police detective. And get this: he was driving a Cadillac!" Anthony stated.

With Gina on his shoulder, Adam could only catch a glimpse of the man. It was enough to make him realize that coming to the funeral home was a big mistake.

"We have to get out of here as quick as possible," he said in an urgent tone.

"What's going on?" Gina asked.

"Quiet!" Adam said. "You're supposed to be unconscious."

"Yeah, and you're supposed to be dead, but I guess nobody's perfect!" she replied.

Anthony led the way through the mass of people standing in the rear hall. He felt like a linebacker at a football game. "Excuse me," he kept saying. It was useless. There were just too many people.

"If we don't get out of here soon, I may really be dead," Adam warned.

Anthony thought for a moment and then had a brainstorm.

"We have a girl who's going to throw up!" he yelled to the mass of humanity.

It was a stroke of genius. The crowd parted like the Red Sea.

"Never doubt the power of vomit!" Anthony pointed out.

"It may be true," Gina said.

"What may be true?" Adam asked.

"If you don't put me down soon, I *am* going to throw up!"

"Yeah, well, throw up on Anthony. It would make him smell better!" Adam snickered.

Anthony wasn't laughing. He had just spotted Mr. Cadillac Cop entering the rear hall.

"I think we better move faster," Anthony stressed. "Yo, Adam, what did you do to that guy? Make fun of his nose or something?"

Suddenly, an old man appeared in front of them. "This way, boys," he said. He ran to a side door and urged them inside. "Hurry, Adam!" he yelled.

"Do you know that guy?" Anthony asked as they ran toward the door.

"No," Adam replied, "and come to think of it, how did he know I was Adam?" He thought for a second. "Wait a minute. There was this old guy chasing me at the museum. It must be him!" Adam realized that he no longer had to carry Gina and quickly put her down. "Gina, go pull that fire alarm thing on the wall over there!"

"Are you crazy?" she asked.

"Yeah, I'm crazy about you. Now *do it*!"

Within seconds, the air was filled with the sounds of ringing and people screaming and shouting.

"Reminds me of dinner at your house," Adam said to Anthony.

"Very funny!" Anthony replied.

"Come on, guys, let's go!" Gina commanded.

"Who died and left you boss?" Adam asked.

"*You did*!" Gina replied. "Now let's get out of here before we get trampled over."

Anthony found a door that led to the rear parking lot. "This way!" he shouted.

The chaos within the funeral parlor had made its way to the outer parking lot. Some people were running in search of cars; others were just running. Adam, Anthony, and Gina blended in with the crowd. To add to the confusion, fire trucks began to arrive. It was a perfect getaway.

"Where to now?" Gina asked.

"Valley Burgers," Adam replied.

"Valley Burgers?" Gina asked. "Why Valley Burgers?"

"Because I'm hungry!" Adam stated. "And if I may make a tiny suggestion: you should stay away from the fries. They can cause zits, you know."

Gina hit him again.

"You're cute when you're mad," Adam groaned.

Gina hit him again and said, "I hate you, Adam Simmons!"

"Yeah," Adam replied, "I hate you, too, Gina Nana Banana!"

CHAPTER FOURTEEN

Tony sat in the thirtieth row in Gold's Funeral Home, examining the face of every child in attendance. He had observed more than eighty tear-stained mugs before hearing Adam's name yelled from the rear of the chapel. It took him a moment to focus on the exact location. With great effort, he spotted Adam's friend Anthony sitting with a girl. *She must be the one who screamed,* he thought. *The question is–why?* As he surveyed the other children in Anthony's row, he saw no one resembling Adam. The scope would have offered him a closer look, but it just wasn't something you would bring to a funeral. If he could just move closer to where Anthony was sitting, perhaps that might help.

He was getting up when he heard the girl yell again. She said something about not being able to live without Adam and then slumped into the arms of an older kid with a mustache who was sitting next to her. The older kid proceeded to picked her up and carry her out of the chapel.

"Somethin' ain't right here," Tony said while making his way to the outer aisle. The trek was slow and arduous. He found himself climbing over hundreds of legs as he struggled to get to the end of the row. Finally, after murmuring his apologies to every mourner in his path, he was free. He watched as Anthony and the girl on the shoulders of the mustached kid left through the rear doors of the chapel. Tony didn't want to draw attention by running up the aisle, but he did his best to try to catch up to them. Just as he reached the rear doors, all hell broke loose. The fire alarm sounded. Between the fire bells, the sirens, and the strobe lights, it was like being in a war zone. Hundreds of chaotic people were screaming and running in every direction. Tony couldn't see more than five feet in front of him. When he did manage to see through the crowd, there was no evidence of his prey. They had simply disappeared. Once again, Tony would be facing his boss with a lame excuse.

Leaning impatiently against a brick wall, Tony cursed his luck while waiting forty-five long minutes before the fire marshal issued the "all clear" and finally allowed people to retrieve their cars from the parking lot. His stomach was churning by the time he started the ignition. The onerous task of navigating the sea of cars in the packed lot had increased his hunger pangs tenfold. By the time he reached the exit, Tony's stomach was making more of a racket than all of the horns that were honking behind him. As he attempted a left onto Hunting Pike, he narrowly missed an old man who was standing aimlessly on the sidewalk.

"Move outta the way, bud!" he screamed to the elderly gentleman.

The man turned, walked over to Tony's car, and rapped on the driver's window. Reluctantly, Tony rolled down the window before he realized whom he had almost run over.

"Why, Mr. Tony," the gray-haired gentleman said, "what a pleasant surprise to see you here. I didn't know you knew the deceased. Too bad the service was disrupted by the fire alarm. It was very upsetting, to say the least. You didn't by any chance see that young boy who seems to elude you? What was his name again? Adam?"

Tony's stomach answered with a growl.

"It sounds to me like you have a slight problem with that stomach of yours. You know, stress is a major contributor of gastric distress. Perhaps you should seek professional help. Maybe this would be a good opportunity to take a vacation. Oh well, look at the time. I have so many things to do today, and chatting with you wasn't on my schedule. Have a nice day!"

Tony waited for him to leave before pounding the steering wheel. "What the hell was that guy, Mr. Irving, doing here?" he screamed. He used his cell phone to make an unpleasant call.

"Boss, this is Tony. We need to talk. There's this place, Aldo's, that has the best grub in town. I'll wait for you there. Oh, by the way, boss, you don't have to wear red pants unless you plan on eatin' meatballs without a napkin!"

"What are you talking about?" the boss asked.

"I dunno. I think a guy by the name Kung Fu said that. It's pretty funny, ain't it?"

"No, it's not. I hope you have something of value to tell me. You are taxing my patience," the boss replied.

"Don't worry, boss, you ain't going to have to pay that tax either."

"Tony, your wit never ceases to amaze me."

"Thanks, boss. I'll see you at the restaurant."

CHAPTER FIFTEEN

"Welcome to Valley Burgers. May I take your order?" asked a tall, lanky, pimply faced, red-haired adolescent wearing a silly cap.

"Yeah, I'll have a Big Valley Burger, Mountain Fries, and a Coke. She'll have a grilled chicken, no fries, and a Diet Coke. And he's having a Little Valley Cheeseburger!" Adam replied.

"I'm not having a Little Valley Cheeseburger!" Anthony quickly interjected.

"I'm sorry," Adam said to the counter person. "Scratch the Little Valley Cheeseburger, and make that a Little Valley Burger without cheese!"

The red-headed geek behind the counter started to giggle.

"I'm not having that either," Anthony said. "You're not funny, Adam."

Adam pointed to the counter person. "Well, he thinks I'm funny."

"What does he know? He works at Valley Burger," Anthony replied.

"You know the difference between him and you?" Adam pointed out. "He has a job, and all you have is bad breath!"

"Will you two cut it out?" Gina shouted. "I thought we came here to eat!"

"I'm trying to place the order, but he keeps changing his mind," Adam replied.

Gina elbowed him again; this time, hard enough to make Adam gasp in pain.

"He's having a Big Valley Burger, Mountain Fries, and a Coke." Adam was hopping up and down, trying to shudder back the pain, as he wheezed the revised order to the giggling geek.

Anthony saw the weird way Adam was moving and said to the geek, "Instead of a Coke, I think I'll have a shake."

Within a minute, Gina was carrying the tray of food to one of the back tables. "I can't wait to hear why you're not dead," she said to Adam.

"Well, I'm sorry to disappoint you, but I don't quite understand it myself," Adam replied.

"I'll tell her," Anthony said. "His father pushed him out the window, he came to my house, Ginger ate the note, and then he stole my bike, and now a tall, ugly guy with a big nose who says he's a cop but drives a Cadillac is looking for him!"

"*What*?" Gina asked.

Anthony tried to explain, but Adam stopped him.

"Look, Gina, there's more to it than that," Adam said. "There's something seriously wrong here."

"I'll say," Gina replied. "Both of you have serious mental issues!"

"Issues?" Anthony asked. "I thought that was a girl thing."

"I don't know what kind of drugs you two are doing, but it's making both of you wacko!" Gina pointed out.

"That's it!" Adam bellowed.

"What's it?" Anthony and Gina asked in unison.

"Drugs! It's about drugs!"

Anthony and Gina expressed a look of confusion.

"Don't you see?" Adam explained. "My mom told me that she caught a kid at the high school doing drugs. She must have told my dad. He was checking it out."

"Yes, so what does that have to do with him throwing you out the window?" Gina asked.

"His father didn't throw him out the window—he *pushed* him out the window," Anthony stated.

"Okay, his father *pushed* him out the window. I still don't see the connection," Gina replied.

"Will you guys listen for a second?" Adam begged. "I don't know why my dad pushed me out the window. Maybe he knew I was in danger. That's why he didn't want me to go to Anthony's house."

"Hold it!" Anthony interrupted. "What was that about not coming to my house?"

"My dad was afraid that it would place you in danger," Adam said.

"When did he tell you that?" Anthony asked.

"It was in the note," Adam said.

"The note that Ginger ate?" Gina asked.

"Yeah, I read part of the note before his dog had it for breakfast," Adam replied.

"Great! Now I'm in danger!" Anthony remarked.

"You were in danger when you decided to eat that Big Valley Burger, Mountain Fries, and a shake. Imagine what that is doing to your arteries right now!" Adam responded.

"Stop it, you two!" Gina demanded. "Adam, you have to try to remember. Did your father say anything else to you? Did he give you anything?"

"Just the note, bag of clothes, his wallet... and, oh yeah, my Gameboy," Adam replied.

"Which doesn't work," Anthony interjected.

"You broke my Gameboy?" Adam asked angrily.

"I didn't break it. It was broken when you gave it to me," Anthony answered.

"Cut it out, you two! You're like a bunch of girls! Listen, Adam, you mentioned a wallet. What was in the wallet?"

Adam retrieved the wallet from his back pocket and threw it on the table. "Just your average old brown leather wallet," he stated.

"Did you check its contents?" Anthony asked.

"No, I just thought I would carry it in my back pocket for the next seventy years. Of course I checked it. All I found were these credit cards, some money, and a business card from an accounting firm."

"That's it?" Anthony asked.

"Oh yeah, I forgot, there was that naked picture of your mother!" Adam added.

"Can't you be serious for once?" Gina asked.

"Sure, I can be serious," Adam answered. "There's this guy with a big nose chasing after me along with this old man who now wants me dead, too!"

"What old man?" Anthony asked.

"The old man who tried to lure us into that room at the funeral home. I think he was the same man at the museum," Adam replied.

"The museum?" Gina asked.

"Yes. Where did you think I got this great disguise?" Adam replied.

"I thought you bought it at Spies-R-Us," Anthony jested.

"Come on, guys, I thought we were going to be serious here," Gina said. "Adam, can you remember anything else that your father told you?"

Adam put his hands up to his brows. "No, I can't remember. You want me to be serious? Okay, here's serious. Do you know what's worse than being chased by two guys who want to kill you?"

"No. What?" Gina asked.

Adam's voice was choked with emotion. He held his hands over his eyes to shield them from his friends. "I never got a chance to tell my parents how much I loved them. And now it's too late!"

CHAPTER SIXTEEN

Tony had selected a roomy booth situated in a quiet corner at the rear of Aldo's restaurant. Ashley, the dancing waitress, glided to the table with a complimentary glass of homemade wine.

"When I'm finished, I'll take another one of these, doll face," he said in a slightly flirtatious fashion.

Ashley didn't know whether to hit him or laugh at him. She didn't mind cute little remarks as long as they weren't from ugly older men with big noses. She realized that she would be guaranteed a bigger tip if she didn't hit him. Of course, an accidental spill might be very appropriate. Ashley smiled and retired to the kitchen for the second glass of homemade wine.

Before drinking the initial glass of wine, Tony held it to the light. The wine was a cloudy shade of red. He wondered whether the cloudiness was from the color of the grapes or from the dirty feet that might have stomped on them. With one large gulp, he downed the entire contents. After producing an enormous belch, he gestured to Ashley for the second glass. She waited a minute, hoping the bad-smelling air would dissipate, before tap dancing her way to the table with the wine.

"Would you like a menu, sir?" she asked.

He winked at her and said, "What I like ain't on the menu!"

Ashley instantly decided that Mr. Big Nose would definitely get spilled on today. Without confrontation, she danced back to the kitchen for a menu and a good laugh.

Tony had just consumed the contents of the second glass when he noticed his boss walking through the door. "Yo, boss, I'm over here," he shouted in a slightly slurred tone.

The boss was wearing a perfectly tailored gray suit with an open-collared black silk shirt ending in French cuffs with shiny gold cuff links. He was definitely overdressed for lunch at Aldo's.

"Hey, boss, you gotta try this wine. It ain't bad for homemade. The girl says it's complimentary, but I think it tastes like Chianti. Anyways, who cares? It's free!"

"How many of those have you had?" the boss asked.

"Just two," Tony slurred, "but don't worry, there's still plenty left for you."

He signaled to Ashley. "Hey, doll, two vinos for my friend over here, and bring over another menu."

Ashley eyed the distinguished-looking gentleman sitting next to Mr. Big Nose and wondered how they could possibly be friends.

"Boss, you can't believe the food in this joint. It's made by a Chinese guy."

"So this is a Chinese restaurant?" the boss asked.

"Nah, Italian," Tony replied. "Don't ya see them checkered tablecloths? That's somethin' you don't find in a Chinese joint. This Chinese guy can make meatballs better than your mama!"

Up until this moment, the boss had had only a mild dislike for Tony, but after the mama insult Tony moved up another rung on the I'm-really-beginning-to-hate-you ladder.

"So, Tony, do you have anything to say to me besides insulting my mother?"

"Yeah, boss, it's about this girl," he replied.

"What girl?"

"This girl I spotted at the funeral home. She was sittin' in the back with that kid, Anthony."

"I'm sure there were many girls attending the funeral. What stoked your curiosity?"

Tony furrowed his eyebrows, attempting to determine the definition of the word *stoked*.

"Why were you interested in this girl?" the boss asked slowly and distinctly enough to satisfy Tony's limited knowledge of the English language.

"She was crying a lot, boss."

"And this is something you find unusual at a funeral?"

"That's not what I meant, boss. This girl, she was really upset about somethin'. She yelled out Adam's name, and then she said somethin' about loving him. And get this boss: she fainted, right there in front of everybody. They had to carry her outta the place. I said to myself, 'Somethin' ain't right about this!' So I tried to check it out."

"What did you do?" asked the boss.

"I went after them, you know, put a tail on them."

"Who exactly did you pursue?"

"I ran up the aisle after the Anthony kid and the guy who was lugging the girl on his shoulders. I almost nabbed them, too, if it wasn't for that stupid fire alarm. Man, you shoulda seen it boss. There were more people screamin' than at one of those Halloween movies. Did you ever see one of those movies, boss?"

"No, I'm afraid that I never had the pleasure. Now, Tony, I know you had an exciting morning, but I would prefer to hear only the relevant information, such as the description of the young lady in question."

"Well, I only saw her for a few seconds before she fainted. She had long, curly hair and this big smile, which I thought was weird because I ain't never seen a girl smile and upset at the same time."

"A big smile, you say?"

"Yeah, boss, she was showin' a bunch of pearly whites."

"I believe the young lady you are describing goes by the name of Gina Nano."

Tony was flabbergasted. How could his boss possibly know this girl?

"Meaning no disrespect, boss, but how did you come up with this girl's name?"

"Mr. Irving revealed it to me," the boss explained.

The very mention of the man's name made the hairs on Tony's arm stand at attention. "Irving? He's an old man, an accountant, for cripes' sake. How would he know about this girl?" Tony demanded.

"It appears that Mr. Irving's talents extend far past the ability of accounting. Unlike you, he has remarkable investigative skills. He attended the funeral today in the hope of uncovering additional information leading to the whereabouts of Adam."

"But, boss, that's my job," Tony argued.

Just then Ashley appeared. "Can I take your order now?" she asked.

"Yeah, yeah, bring some of them meatballs, a calzone, and a plate of lasagna," Tony ordered. He turned to his boss. "You want anything, boss?"

"No," his boss chuckled, "I'll just sit here and watch you eat. Maybe I'll just nibble a bit from your plate."

"Better make it two orders of meatballs," Tony instructed Ashley and then rudely waved her off.

"So, boss, like I was saying…"

The boss held up his hand to stop Tony's incessant ramblings. "I have to wash my hands. Hold that thought for a moment, Tony."

On the way back from the men's room, the boss peered through the little window on the door leading to the kitchen. From Tony's description, he had envisioned a Chinese chef with a meat cleaver in his hand, busily chopping Italian spices. Instead, there was a non-Asian old lady carefully stirring sauce in a ten-gallon pot. He couldn't wait to hear Tony's stupid explanation about that.

Tony's stomach refused to wait five minutes for the boss to return. No sooner did Ashley bring the food to the table than Tony was shoveling meatballs and pasta into his mouth.

"It looks like you are enjoying this impressive culinary banquet," the boss commented.

Tony looked up from his plate and said, "I don't know about any calamari, but these meatballs are damn good!"

The boss shook his head in an effort to clear Tony's last stupid response. He tried one of the meatballs and found it a true epicurean delight. It indeed was better than his mother's.

"So this food was prepared by a person of Asian descent?" he asked Tony.

"Na, a Chinese guy, like I told ya," Tony replied. "He owns the joint."

"I see," replied the boss. "And this person does all the cooking?"

"Yeah, boss, only him."

At that moment, Aldo entered the restaurant. He was holding bags of fresh vegetables. Tony stood to attract his attention.

"Yo, Aldo, come here. I want ya to meet one of my friends."

After placing the bags in the kitchen, Aldo joined Tony at the table. The boss rose to shake Aldo's hand.

"A pleasure to meet you, sir," he said to Aldo. "Tony has explained to me that you do all the cooking. Is that true?"

"Do you believe everything that your friend says?" Aldo asked.

The boss thought for a moment and then answered, "Not everything."

"Then you are truly not his friend," Aldo smiled and shook the boss's hand. "We share something in common. It is my pleasure to meet you, sir."

Aldo then retired to the kitchen. Tony was very confused. He ate another meatball.

"I like this man, Aldo," the boss said.

Tony frowned. There was red sauce dripping from the corner of his mouth. "Yeah, well, I used to like him, but he just kinda made me look a little stupid."

"Don't worry, Tony, I don't think that you are just a *little* stupid."

Tony smiled. He took it as a compliment.

"So, boss, do you want me to grab the girl?"

"No. I don't think that is necessary," he replied.

"But ain't she important?"

"It is not your concern," he explained to Tony. "Mr. Irving is handling that matter."

The color of Tony's face now matched the red sauce that dripped from his lips. His dislike for Mr. Irving instantly escalated to real hatred.

"But the guy's an accountant, for cripes' sake," Tony pleaded.

"There's no need to repeat yourself. You mentioned that fact to me earlier."

"But, boss…"

The boss waved Tony to silence. Tony wasn't about to let Mr. Irving handle something that should be left to a professional. Regardless of what his boss thought, Tony could grab the girl and make her talk, even if that meant working her over. He knew he was capable. He would show the boss that he was no dummy.

"Whatever you say. You're the boss," he said.

Tony picked up the calzone and attempted to shove it into his mouth. The boss decided to end their little lunch meeting by seeking asylum through the exit doors. When Tony finished devouring his food, he asked for the bill and then gave Ashley a ten-dollar tip, not nearly enough to cover all his abuse.

"Tell Aldo I wanna see him, doll face," he demanded.

Aldo appeared immediately. "Was everything to your satisfaction?" he asked.

"No, it ain't!" Tony bellowed. "You made me look like a fool in front of my boss."

Aldo thought for a moment and replied, "My apologies for making you look like a fool. That is a job best suited for a mirror!"

Ashley carried a pitcher of water to Tony's table. "Would you like some water?" she asked.

"Sure, doll, I like anything you give me."

Ashley gave him her biggest smile and proceeded to fill Tony's glass to the brim. As he lifted the overly filled glass to his mouth, she accidentally on purpose bumped his arm.

"Have a nice day!" she said and danced back to the kitchen.

CHAPTER SEVENTEEN

Adam had dried his fifteenth car of the morning. Two days ago, he had secured a job at the American Car Wash, not because he needed money, but for the information he sought. He knew of the township's policy to keep all the police cars clean and spotless. Housed in each police car was a portable computer that could access the picture database of known criminals. If Adam could get his hands on one of those computers, he might be able to gather some information on the identities of the big-nosed, Cadillac-driving maniac and the seemingly innocent but relentless old man. Unfortunately, Mr. Willard, the owner of the car wash, had other ideas. He thought that the best use of Adam's fingers were behind two soft terrycloth towels.

As each dirty four-wheeled vehicle crawled its way through the tunnel of soap suds, scrubbers, flashing red and green lights, hot wax, and finally the high-power blower, Adam hoped to see a freshly scrubbed police car emerge. His plan was simple yet effective. All he had to do was spray window cleaner on the interior windows, which would make it impossible for anyone to actually observe his true intentions.

Another twenty cars later, Adam's wish was granted. A shiny Crown Victoria, complete with a bar of red emergency beacons attached to the roof, rolled his way. He waved his arms and signaled Mr. Willard in a fashion indicating that he required no assistance in drying the squad car.

Taking long, fast strides, he approached the car with a large orange bucket in hand containing the necessary drying paraphernalia: spray cans of tire and window cleaners, two soft drying towels, and a tiny spray bottle of air freshener to provide that new-car smell.

He dried the Crown Vic with a vigor only found in youth. Great detail was spent making sure that the tires, wheel wells, and door jambs were dry and dirt-free. Not one drop of water remained on the car's exterior. His heart raced as he opened the doors and moved to clean the interior.

Within minutes there was a thick film of white foam covering all the inside glass. Positive of his cloaking maneuver, he pulled out the little tray that held the computer's keyboard. He manipulated the keys like a professional, but to his chagrin, he found that a user password was required. His feeble attempts of random entries yielded the same response: Access denied. Frustrated, he opened the glove compartment in the hope of finding an operation manual that might contain a default password that the computer might still consider valid. No such luck. All he found was registration and insurance information. His efforts were thwarted by a single little word. He would just have to wait for the next Crown Vic with red lights on its roof.

Resolving to clean the foam from the interior windows, Adam noticed that the police radio was turned off. Assuming that there might be some interesting chatter on the police band, he flipped the switch to the on position. Hearing nothing but white noise, he adjusted the radio's squelch knob until it reached the silent threshold. Suddenly, the dispatcher's voice emerged from the little squawk speaker located near the floor. It was a woman speaking in short, crisp, authoritative tones, giving an information directive. Apparently, a mother had called in about her daughter who apparently hadn't come home last night. "Boy, is she in trouble," Adam said to himself.

Noticing a uniformed patrolman marching over to retrieve his shiny car, Adam quickly reached for the switch to shut off the radio. He was about to flip it down when the dispatcher's voice erupted again with more information concerning the missing girl. She described the girl's height, weight, color of hair, color of eyes, and clothing. She continued with the girl's name. That last tidbit of information was enough to make Adam's spine tingle with fear. The girl was Gina Nano!

Chapter Eighteen

....

The room's odor was a cross between bleach and ammonia.
Although her blindfold had been removed, the pitch-black room
made it impossible for her to see more than three inches in front of her
nose. She could, however, feel the motor vibrations of the machines
that hummed in close proximity. Occasionally, she would hear fluid
flow in the pipes overhead. More than once, she had tried to rise from
the wooden chair, but her hands and feet were firmly bound to its
rungs. Although she wanted to yell, it was not an option because she
was effectively gagged by a piece of cloth that had been placed in her
mouth. Her head throbbed from the residue of the chemicals that had
been used to make her sleep. She had no idea how long she had been
sitting in the darkness. How did she get here? She had to think.

The last thing she remembered was stopping at Valley Burgers for
fries and a Coke after babysitting for little Blake, or Blakey, as he liked
to be called. He was a cute kid who liked to play with his "twains." She
loved the way he cried out in delight as she pushed the trains through
the tunnel. "Do it again," he would say, "do it again!" She couldn't
believe that she was getting paid to make such a cute little kid happy.
She only needed ten more dollars to buy one of those Tiffany bracelets
that dangled from the wrists of all her friends. Another babysitting job
would do it. Life for Gina Nano was great!

She was just sitting there, eating her fries, sipping her Coke,
picturing the silver bracelet on her left wrist, when she felt the need to

visit the bathroom. "I'm coming back," she indicated to the busboy. "Don't touch my fries and Coke!"

She had been gone for only a few minutes. When she returned to the table, she finished the fries and Coke. Eating the fried foods did not make her feel guilty. Despite Adam's teasing, she knew that wouldn't put zits on her face. The next time they got together, she would make sure to show him that there were no pimples on her face worth popping.

Although it was only nine in the evening, she found herself yawning as she left the Valley. She couldn't believe that playing with little Blakey had exhausted her so much. After yawning ten times in a row, she wondered if she might be setting a new Guinness record. Everything appeared to be in slow motion as she continued her trek toward her house. She kept thinking that in ten minutes she would be lying in bed between comfy sheets with Fluffy, her favorite stuffed animal. She was so tired. Her head began to spin, and she had to sit.

"Here, let me help you," she heard someone say. It was the voice of a man, a familiar voice.

"I'm so tired," she tried to say, but the words came out all jumbled.

"Don't worry," he told her. "You just need to sleep."

He picked her up and put her in the car.

"Where are we going?" she tried to say.

"Someplace safe," he answered. "Don't worry, just go to sleep."

Gina smiled and then closed her eyes.

CHAPTER NINETEEN

Tim Faraday sat in his slightly claustrophobic office reviewing the batch of current files that had been placed in the inbox on his desk. The files were always sorted by priority, the top being the most important. Today's top folder had a red Missing Persons label. He considered taking a sip of his cold coffee before proceeding, but after seeing how the curdled cream had formed across its surface, he decided to forego the idea. With great reluctance, he opened the folder containing Gina Nano's name.

The information gathered by the on-scene officer was very sparse, yielding little if any clues. At 9:00 p.m. two evenings ago, Gina Nano was last seen at the Valley Burgers restaurant located on Hunting Pike. Kevin Connel, a Valley employee, stated that he saw Gina sitting at a back booth eating fries and drinking a soda. Before going to the bathroom, she had instructed him not to touch her food; then she returned minutes later, finished her meal, and left. Four patrolmen made a comprehensive door-to-door search within a two-mile radius of the restaurant, but nothing turned up. People on the street were questioned to no avail. Not one person had seen or heard anything. The interrogation of Gina's family and friends obtained no additional information. The manila Missing Persons folder lacked any clues that were deemed worthwhile. Apparently, Gina Nano had walked out of the restaurant and simply disappeared!

Grasping at straws, Faraday looked at the police blotter that listed all the criminal activity that had occurred in the last two weeks. Aside from a few vandalized mailboxes, an act of criminal mischief caused by rebellious adolescents, it had been a pretty quiet period. The only item listed that caught Faraday's attention was the questionable act of arson at the Simmons' residence. He searched his cluttered desk for the notes on the fire. Perhaps there was some connection. Steve Silver, the district justice, might not agree with the legal precedence, but Faraday didn't care. It was time to pull in Tony the Match for questioning.

...

"I'm glad you could make it," Faraday said to Tony.

"Did I have a choice?" Tony replied. "One of your cops pulled me over while I was drivin' to see a sick friend. I was supposed to bring 'em some chicken soup. Ya know, it will be your fault if my friend starves!"

"And what would be the name of this *sick* friend?"

Tony thought for a moment and then replied, "Bubba!"

"His name is Bubba?"

"Yeah," Tony answered. "You gotta problem wid dat?"

"No. Perhaps you could give me his address."

"Whaddaya need his address for?" Tony asked.

"I want to send him a get well card," Faraday said with a smile.

Tony smiled back. "Well, Bubba don't read!"

"That's a shame," Faraday replied. "Perhaps you could answer a few of my questions."

"More questions about Bubba?"

"No, I was going to ask you questions about Gina Nano."

"Who?"

"Gina Nano," Faraday said slowly and distinctly.

"Never heard of the young broad," Tony replied.

"Who said she was young?" Faraday asked. "I just mentioned her name, not her age."

"Yeah, well, I just took a guess," Tony answered.

"Since we are guessing here, can you guess where she might be?"

"What do I look like? Her fairy godmother or somethin'? Maybe she's wid that boyfriend of hers—Adam."

Tony regretted that statement the second the words left his mouth.

"Adam?" Faraday asked. "Now how would you know her boyfriend's name?"

"You're the one who told me to guess. I guess I'm a good guesser!"

"You said that maybe she was with her boyfriend, Adam. Did you know that Adam died in a fire?"

"Yeah, that's what everybody says."

"You know about the fire?" Faraday asked.

"Yeah, I know about it. So what? That don't mean nothin'!"

"Where were you on the night of the fire?" Faraday asked.

"I was with a friend!"

"And just who might that friend be?"

"Bubba!" Tony smiled.

"Was this the sick friend you mentioned earlier?"

"Nah, it was another friend named Bubba!"

"Another friend named Bubba—that's very interesting."

"Yeah, I call all my friends Bubba. I'd call you Bubba, but you ain't my friend."

"You mentioned that everybody thinks that Adam is dead. Do you think that, also?"

"Who cares what I think?" Tony fidgeted in his chair. "Look, I gotta go. I got a doctor's appointment."

"Are you sick?" Faraday asked.

"Nah, I'm thinkin' about gettin' my nose fixed. It kinda makes me look mean. I'm really a sweet person, ya know."

"I only have a few more questions," Faraday stated.

"Well, make it snappy. I hate makin' a doctor wait. It just ain't right to make a doctor wait!"

Faraday chuckled. "You're a funny man. You should be a comedian."

"Yeah, well, I ain't quittin' my day job."

"And what job would that be?"

"I sell Girl Scout cookies."

"Are you going to be honest with any of your answers?"

"Okay, ya got me. I don't sell Girl Scout cookies."

"Let's get back to Gina Nano for the moment. Do you know where she might be?"

"Maybe she's at the dentist, workin' on that big smile of hers."

Faraday lifted his eyebrow slightly. "So you know what she looks like?"

Tony fidgeted once again. "Look, all I know is that you ain't got no right to harass me like this."

"I'm not harassing you, I'm just asking you some friendly questions."

"Yeah, well, you ain't my friend, and I ain't answering any more questions!"

"You refuse to answer any more questions?"

Tony didn't reply. He just sat there as if his ears no longer worked.

"I guess that will be all for right now," Faraday finally said.

Tony laughed as he left the room.

CHAPTER TWENTY

"Quick, get out! You must get out now!"

A thick black smoke was beginning to blanket the room. He could barely breathe. He kept hearing the voice, but try as he might, he couldn't determine its location.

"Hurry... before it's too late." The voice was so familiar. He attempted to concentrate, but his mind kept drifting. Something was wrong. Maybe it was the toxic smoke. He had to snap out of it.

"Dad?" he managed to call out. "Is that you?"

"Hurry, you have to leave. You must get out now!" the voice repeated.

It was his dad. Although he couldn't see through the smoke, he was almost positive. "Dad, what's happening? Where's Mom, Dad?"

"There's no time for conversation. You must leave now!"

He peered through the blackness and attempted to reach out toward the voice. "Dad, do you know that Gina is missing?"

"Yes, but don't worry about her," the voice replied. "Just follow me."

He found the strength to walk. Although he couldn't see where he was going, he put one foot in front of the other and followed the voice.

"Over here," beckoned the voice, "I'm over here."

He could make out the silhouette of a figure standing by a door in the distance. The smoke seemed thinner near the door.

"This way," the voice pleaded, "come this way."

Everything was in slow motion. He could see the person waving to him.

"Dad, is that you?" he screamed as he continued through the black void.

"This way, come this way!"

He was closer now, close enough to recognize the person standing by the door. It was an old man. He was so confused. It sounded like his dad, but the voice came from an old man. It was a trap.

"No!" he shouted. "I'm not going with you."

"You must listen to me," the voice said.

"I don't have to listen to you," he called out, his voice choked with emotion. "You're not my father! You're just trying to trick me!"

He watched as the man disappeared through the door.

Adam cried like he'd never cried before. He was all alone in the dark. His parents were dead, people were coming after him, he had placed his friends in danger, and now Gina was missing. It was his fault. "Why are these things happening to me?" he cried.

Suddenly, there was a noise, a ringing sound, in the distance. It was soft at first, but now it was getting louder. It was an obnoxious sound, too loud to ignore. It seemed like it was right next to his left ear. "Stop ringing!" he shouted, but it continued, over and over again.

He had to do something. With his left hand, he reached out to the sound, and without thinking, he pushed a button.

"Adam?" he heard. It was a tinny voice coming from where the ringing had stopped. "Adam, are you there?" said the familiar voice. It belonged to Anthony.

Adam opened his eyes. He was lying in a bed, and sweat was pouring from his face.

"Hello? Adam, are you there?"

Adam brought the little cell phone to his ear. He tried to shake the cobwebs from his brain. "Anthony, is that you?" he asked.

"Of course it's me. Don't you remember? I gave you my mom's cell phone. I told her that I left it at a friend's house. You can't keep it, you know. And another thing: I want my bike back! What's wrong with you, Adam? You sound weird."

"Nothing is wrong. You just woke me up from a nightmare, that's all."

"A nightmare? No kidding. Was it about vampires? I always dream about vampires. Did you ever notice that female vampires have big hooters?"

Adam chuckled. "For a little kid, you're a big pervert. You know that, Anthony?"

"Yeah," he replied proudly, "I am!"

"So what do you want?" Adam asked.

"What do you mean?" Anthony replied.

"You called me, remember? Stop thinking about hooters, and tell me why you called."

"It's about Gina," Anthony said.

"What about her?"

"I think I know what happened to her."

"You do? Well, tell me quick before I come over to your house and beat you with your mother's cell phone!"

"Okay, okay, calm down. She was kidnapped."

"No kidding. You are a real Sherlock Holmes. Of course she was kidnapped. You've got to be stupid to think she got lost walking home from Valley Burgers. Tell me something I don't know."

"Okay, I will. She was kidnapped by the old man!"

"The old man?" Adam asked.

"Yeah, the old man who tried to catch us at the funeral home. He kidnapped her, and he's going to kill her!"

"Slow down. No one is killing anybody," Adam replied.

"That's easy for you to say. You're hiding out in the Bryn Athyn Museum. Nobody even knows you're alive. I, on the other hand, am a sitting duck just waiting to be shot!"

"Who's shooting at you?" Adam asked.

"That guy who drives the Cadillac. He probably has a gun bigger than his fat, ugly nose. He's been to my house. One day, I'm going to open the door and he's going to be standing there with a .357 Magnum. He's a killer, I know he is."

"You know what I think, Anthony?"

"What, Adam?"

"You've been watching way too much television. Like I said, nobody is killing anybody."

"You really think that, Adam?"

"I don't think it, I know it. If someone wanted us dead, they would have done it already."

"Maybe they tried but they weren't successful," Anthony pointed out.

"Okay, smart guy, tell me when they tried."

Anthony thought for a moment. "When they set your house on fire, okay. They got your parents, and now they're coming after you and your friends."

Adam knew Anthony might be right, but he refused to admit it. "Why, Anthony? Tell me why."

"Hey, I'm just a dumb kid. You're the one with the brains. There has to be a clue somewhere. We can't just wait until they kill Gina. I'm going crazy here with nothing to do."

"Nothing to do? You have a computer, a television, and my Gameboy. How can you have nothing to do? I'm lying here in a dusty old bed, hiding in a museum that creeks in the middle of the night. The way I see it, you have nothing to complain about."

"Yeah, I have something to complain about: your Gameboy doesn't work!"

"Well, it worked before you stole it out of my backpack, and it better work when you return it, or else you'll never see your bike again. Did you check the batteries?"

"Duh, why didn't I think of that? Of course I checked the batteries," Anthony replied. "I may be a pervert, but I know about video games. The batteries aren't the problem."

"Then the problem must be you," Adam stated. "Forget the Gameboy for a second and listen to me. Why don't we meet at Valley Burgers tomorrow in the morning? We'll ask a few questions. Maybe we will find a clue."

"Don't you think the police already did that?"

"Of course they did, but we're kids; we have a different way of looking at things. What do we have to lose?"

"Our lives, for one thing," Anthony stated. "We could be kidnapped, just like Gina!"

"Look on the bright side. If that happens, the puzzle is solved. We'll find out who the kidnapper is, and we'll find Gina!"

"Yeah, and I'll be dead!" Anthony complained.

"No great loss," Adam retorted. "Now stop whining!"

CHAPTER TWENTY-ONE

The smell of money was in the air. Patrons of all ages were huddled over pulp-enhanced orange juice made from concentrate, and "freshly brewed" hour-old coffee with a hint of hazelnut. They were busy reading newspapers while attempting to consume breakfast specials consisting of a combination of artery-clogging fats and simple carbohydrates. Some plates were topped with pancakes smothered in hydrogenated margarine and imitation maple syrup. Others had a more balanced fare consisting of muffin specials filled with fried eggs, bacon, and processed cheese with a side order of home fries resembling a frozen, shredded potato patty that had been dropped in a vat of oil for three minutes. Diners were busy shoveling in their first meal of high-fat, high-calorie food as fast as their forks could hit their mouths, and they loved it. It was a typical morning at Valley Burgers.

An assembly line of people moved from the ordering counter to the pick-up area to the final destination, which was a bright yellow dining room filled with multicolored plastic tables and chairs. If you were lucky, you would find yourself sitting in a large booth recently vacated by a mother and her three children who had decorated the table with crayoned stick people, jelly, and crumbs of whatever happened to have missed their mouths. Adam and Anthony were deemed lucky this day. They sat in style as they watched the typical American indulge in what had become the new breakfast of champions.

"Oh, before I forget, here's your mom's cell phone," Adam said.

"What about my bike? When do I get that back?" Anthony asked.

"Hey, don't push it, you little twerp."

"Okay, okay, but you are going to return it, right?"

"Sure. Yikes, look over there!"

Anthony strained to see where Adam was pointing. And there he was, standing at the front counter, ordering breakfast: none other than Mr. Big Nose.

"What are we going to do?" he asked Adam.

Adam scanned the rear dining room in search of a fast exit. All he could find were two doors. One was an emergency fire door, which had a sign indicating that an alarm would sound if someone opened it; the other was a red kitchen door marked "Employees only." "How do you feel about working for Valleys?" he asked.

"We're about to be killed by Big Nose over there, and you're interested in getting a job at Valleys? What, are you crazy?"

"No, I just like the benefits," Adam answered.

"What benefits?"

Adam pointed to the two doors. "We can't go out the emergency door because an alarm will sound, so that leaves us with the one marked 'Employees only.'"

"Great choice. Now what do we do?"

"Just do whatever I do." Adam started folding his paper placemat.

Very confused while following Adam's instructions, Anthony asked, "Let me guess: We're making paper airplanes so we can fly out of here?"

"Nah," Adam replied and continued folding.

"Okay, we're making paper knives to defend ourselves?"

"Will you stop being stupid? We're making hats!"

"Oh, we're making hats. That makes sense. Can we make coats when we're finished? Pardon me for being stupid, but why are we making hats?"

Adam placed his finished hat on his head. The words "Valley Burgers" were displayed across the front. "How do I look?" he asked.

"All you need are some pimples on your face, and you'll blend right in," Anthony replied with a laugh. He quickly donned his masterpiece. "What now?"

"We pick up our trays and walk through the kitchen door."

"Sounds like a plan to me." Anthony grabbed his tray and led the way. "I always wanted to work at Valleys. You get free food, you know."

"Don't forget about the health benefits," Adam pointed out.

"Health benefits?"

"You'll be happy you have health benefits after eating all the free food!"

The employee door led to a long white tiled room containing brooms, mops, and spray cleaner. They continued to the far end where there was another door. They opened it a crack and peeked in. An army of teenagers was engaged in various skills, ranging from flipping burgers to secretly flipping the finger to the store manager, who was yelling at everyone to move faster.

"What do we do now?" Anthony asked quietly.

"Grab two of those mops over there. We're going to mop our way through the kitchen, right out the back door."

It was a great plan—providing they weren't seen by the store manager. They shuttled into the kitchen with their heads down and their mops moving from side to side. The short, moderately obese, acne-scarred french fry machine operator threw them a puzzled look. Everyone in the kitchen was wearing a white Valley Burgers smock, complete with bright red trim. Adam and Anthony's attire was not in compliance. They quickly continued toward the rear door. Only twenty more feet remained to freedom.

"What are you two doing?" screamed the manager. "Why aren't you in uniform?"

The two boys abandoned their mops and made a run for the exit door.

"Stop!" yelled the manager.

Tony, "Mr. Big Nose," had just finished placing his order when he heard the screaming. Because of the open kitchen design, he could see the two boys running toward the back door. He caught enough of a glimpse to recognize Anthony, and he guessed that Adam was the other boy.

Tony threw his tray to the side and ran out the front door. He turned the corner and headed to the rear of the building. Spotting Adam and Anthony running down the rear alley, he pursued at top speed, but they were younger and faster. He had to do something to slow them down, so he pulled out his gun, took aim, and fired. The shot was wide and to the right. Normally, he was an expert shot, but this was the first time he had ever used his gun while running. He fired again, and the bullet ricocheted off the pavement, just slightly to the left of Anthony.

"What the heck was that?" Anthony yelled to his friend.

Adam continued to run, but turned his head enough to see a nightmare in progress. "You don't want to know," he replied. "Don't run in a straight line. We have to zigzag."

"Are you crazy?" Anthony asked.

"No, Mr. Big Nose is! And he's shooting at us!"

"I knew it, I knew it. Didn't I tell you?"

"Okay, you're right. Does that make you feel better? When he kills you, I'll make sure your gravestone says, 'Here lies Anthony—he's right'!"

Tony shot again, and the bullet whizzed by Anthony's head.

"Maybe we should split up. That way, he can't shoot us both," Adam shouted.

They came to the end of the alley. As Adam went to the left, he motioned Anthony to the right. Another bullet bounced off the concrete right behind Anthony's foot. Crazy Mr. Big Nose was closing in. Adam watched as Anthony ran into the street, waving his hands and screaming for help. A car stopped, and the driver rolled down his window and yelled for Anthony to get in. Anthony yanked open the passenger door and jumped into the car to avoid the next bullet. Adam couldn't believe Anthony's luck. What were the odds of a car stopping to help? As he ran, he thought more about the car. *Why was it there?* He then realized who was driving the car—the old man! Anthony had jumped into the hands of the kidnapper!

CHAPTER TWENTY-TWO

Adam spent the next three hours trying to decide what to do next. At first, he was angry; angry for the death of his parents, angry for being careless with his father's note, angry for telling Gina he was alive and getting her involved, and angry for placing both the lives of Anthony and Gina in danger. It would have been better if he had died in the fire. If that had happened, his friends would not be in jeopardy.

After beating himself up over the situation in which he was placed, Adam decided that it was up to him to help his friends. He must act quickly. He would do whatever it took, and he would do it alone.

Using his skills of reasoning, he deduced that there was a way to find Anthony and, hopefully, Gina. The key was the cell phone that he had returned to Anthony. It seemed simple enough. All he had to do was call Anthony and ask where he was. Thankfully, he scratched that idea. If the kidnapper heard the phone ring, he would snatch it from Anthony and smash it to the ground. He might get very angry and hurt Anthony. No, Adam couldn't call. He had to use the phone another way, but how? Maybe he could find out the cell phone's location by tracking it.

He remembered a conversation he once had with his father about how a driver in distress used his cell phone to call 9-1-1. The police were somehow able to determine where the broken-down car was located. His father mentioned something about triangulation. Adam didn't know exactly how triangles would be helpful, but he was sure the cell phone company had the answer. He jumped on his bike and quickly pedaled to the nearest cell phone store.

"Hi, my name is Anthony Trent," he lied, "and I have a big problem."

The man behind the counter was wearing a red shirt and sporting a big white beard and an even bigger stomach. For a moment, Adam thought Santa Claus held a side job as a Huntingdon Valley cell phone salesman. "A big problem, you say? Well, it's your lucky day. I like big problems. Let me see your cell phone. I can fix anything."

"That's one of the problems: I lost it!"

"People lose phones all the time. All we have to do is cancel the number and get a new phone. Do you have cell phone insurance?"

"No, you don't understand. It's not my phone, it belongs to my mom. She's always lecturing me about being responsible, and I lost it. She's going to kill me. Please, you have to help me find it."

"Did you leave the cell phone on?"

"Yes."

"Great! Then all you have to do is call the number. Someone will hear it ring, answer the phone, and with luck you'll get it back."

"I can't do that," Adam quickly replied. "I placed it in silent mode."

"I see. So how do you think I can help you?"

"With triangles," Adam responded.

The Santa Claus clone lifted his eyebrows. "Triangles?"

"No, I meant to say triangulation."

"Ah, triangulation. Now how would you know of triangulation?"

"I saw something about it on TV. Isn't there a way of finding the phone using triangulation?"

"Do you know what triangulation is?"

"Not exactly, but I'm good with math. Does it have something to do with math?"

"As a matter of fact, it does!"

The man took a piece of paper and started drawing. "This dot is a cell phone tower. It has a range of two miles." He had diagrammed a circle with a dot in the center. "All cell phones constantly transmit an ESN identifying code to the tower. As the phone moves from cell tower to cell tower, it transmits its general location."

"But I need to know its exact location. According to your diagram, it could be anywhere within the two-mile range of the tower."

"That's where triangulation comes into play." He drew another dot and circle on the paper. The circle of the second tower slightly overlapped the circle of the first tower. "Using the strength of the cell phone's signal, we can determine the distance of the phone from cell tower one to cell tower two." He pointed to the oval section that had been created by overlapping the two circles. "You see how much closer we are to the phone's location? The more towers we use, the more exact the location. That's what triangulation is all about."

Adam was very excited. This triangulation process was going to work. "Great! Let's do it!"

"Hold on. I didn't say I could do it, I just said it could be done."

"Why can't you do it?" Adam asked with disappointment.

The man pulled out a form from under the counter. "Because we need one of these filled out—an emergency work order form."

Adam grabbed the piece of paper. "Okay, I'll fill out the form."

"And I'll need some identification," the man continued.

"Identification?"

"Sure. How do I know if you are truly Anthony Trent? You could be a serial killer or a stalker."

Adam thought for a moment. "Well, you have to trust me. How do I know you are really a cell phone salesman? You could be Santa Claus."

"Good point," the man replied with a smile, "but that doesn't change the fact that I need identification. You look too young to drive, so that rules out a driver's license. Perhaps you can show me a library card or something like that."

All Adam possessed was his father's wallet, which contained nothing that could help him. "I left my library card at home. How about if you help me fill out the form, and then I'll run home to get it?"

The Santa clone smiled. "Okay, but remember: no triangulation until you return with the library card." He put out his hand, and they shook on the deal.

CHAPTER TWENTY-THREE

The bike ride to Anthony's house was uneventful. Even though the cell phone store was only fifteen minutes away, it took more than a half hour. Adam was getting quite proficient at staying off all the main streets. It was better to be safe than sorry.

Adam hid the bike behind the garage and then carefully climbed the tree outside Anthony's bedroom window. He was as quiet as a church mouse, hoping not to draw the attention of Ginger, the golden retriever. Thankfully, the window was unlocked. Using great care, he pried it open and entered Anthony's humble abode. To his good fortune, the dog was nowhere in sight.

He started at the top dresser drawer and worked his way down, checking under all the clothing, including a ridiculous pair of Spiderman underpants. He couldn't wait until he found Anthony so he could rib him about that. Anthony's closet was a bit more difficult to search. There were more clothes on the floor than on the hangers. Adam couldn't tell what was clean or dirty. Everything sat in piles covering the entire floor. It would have been easier finding a needle in a haystack. He wasn't even sure that Anthony owned a library card.

Realizing that the closet search would take too long, Adam went to Anthony's computer desk. There it was, a Huntingdon Valley Library Card, lying on top of the printer stand right next to his Gameboy. When he reached over to get the card, he accidentally bumped into the computer chair, which edged the printer just enough to knock his

Gameboy to the floor.

"Anthony, is that you?" Mrs. Trent called up to the second floor.

Adam froze in fear.

"Is someone up there?" Mrs. Trent asked in a loud, authoritative yet worried voice.

Adam scurried to the window just as Ginger started barking. For some reason, the window was stuck. Aside from the tornado hit closet, Adam had nowhere to hide.

"I'm calling the police!" Mrs. Trent yelled to Anthony's bedroom.

Adam pushed on the window again, but it wouldn't budge. Then he noticed that when he had closed the window earlier he must have accidently locked it. Without spending another second, he quickly unlocked the latch, opened the window, and jumped to the tree, carelessly scraping his shins and arms as he quickly shimmied down. By the time he reached the hidden bike, he could hear the approaching sirens. Oblivious to the pain from his scrapes, he jumped on the bike and pedaled away through the back woods.

"Good afternoon, Mrs. Trent. I came as quickly as I could."

"Your name is Tim, isn't it?"

"Yes, ma'am, Detective Tim Faraday. You called about a prowler?"

"That's right. I've been pretty jumpy since our last little meeting. Between the fire at the Simmons' house, the visit of that phony policeman with the big nose, and the disappearance of Gina Nano, I'm scared to death. A few minutes ago there was a strange noise coming from Anthony's room. I called up to Anthony, but he didn't answer. Then Ginger started barking. She never barks when Anthony is making noise in his room."

"Are you sure that Anthony is not home?"

"Pretty sure, but I didn't go upstairs to find out. I sat right here waiting for you."

"Maybe I should take a look. Do you mind?"

"Please do," Phyllis Trent replied.

After a few minutes, Detective Faraday called downstairs, "Mrs.

Trent, could you come up here for a second? Don't worry, it's safe."

Phyllis Trent climbed the stairs to Anthony's room. "What did you find?" she asked.

"It appears that someone broke in and ripped apart everything in the closet."

Phyllis opened the closet door, expecting the worse. "Where?" she asked as she looked in.

"Can't you see it? They must have torn everything from the hangers and thrown it on the floor."

For the first time in a while, Phyllis laughed. "You don't have any children, do you, detective?"

"No, ma'am, I don't."

She closed the door. "One day, when you have children, you'll understand about closets!"

Detective Faraday had a sheepish look on his face. "Mrs. Trent—"

"Please call me Phyllis," she interrupted.

"Okay. Phyllis, does anything look out of the ordinary? Was anything taken?"

Phyllis scanned the room. Nothing was missing. Then she spotted it.

"Nothing is missing," she said, "but something is definitely out of the ordinary."

"What do you mean?" Faraday asked.

Phyllis pointed to the Gameboy on the floor.

"The Gameboy?" Faraday questioned. "What is so odd about that?"

"Anthony doesn't own a Gameboy. We weren't going to buy him one until his birthday. Only one of his friends has one."

"And who might that be?" Faraday asked.

"Adam Simmons," she replied with a tear in her eye.

"How did Anthony get it?"

"That is something I would love to ask him."

"Speaking of Anthony, do you know where he is, ma'am?"

"No, I don't. Usually he calls. He's been gone since this morning."

"Where did he go?"

"He said he was going to Valley Burgers."

"What was he wearing?" Faraday asked.

"He was wearing jeans and a red shirt. Why do you ask?"

Detective Faraday tried not to show it, but he had a very bad feeling. A few hours earlier, there had been a report about someone shooting at two boys who had been running behind the rear of the Valleys. One of the boys was wearing clothes matching those worn by Anthony Trent.

CHAPTER TWENTY-FOUR

"Hello, is anybody here?" Adam asked.

"I'll be with you in a second," a voice called out from the back room.

Adam's heart was still pounding from the high-speed bike ride. He was so mad. *I'm the worst burglar in the world,* he thought. He reached into his pocket and withdrew the library card. To his chagrin, it had expired two months ago. *Cripes, Anthony, can't you cut me a break here? I'm trying to help you. Couldn't you have a valid library card?*

The jovial Santa Claus double magically appeared at the front counter.

"Hello there, Anthony."

Adam was staring at the expired library card.

"Is something wrong?"

Adam looked up. "No. I just realized that I forgot to renew my library card. I hope it won't be a problem."

"Not for me," the Santa clone replied. "Of course, I'm not the one who has to use it at the library."

"Yeah, I guess I'm kind of stupid," Adam said with a silly look on his face as he handed over the library card.

"Let's see. You lost your mother's cell phone, and you forgot to renew your library card. I wouldn't call you stupid, a little irresponsible and forgetful, but definitely not stupid! Here's your form, all filled out. Just give it a John Hancock, and we'll be ready for the next stage."

"A John Hancock? What's that?"

"Your signature. You've never heard of that before? John Hancock signed the Constitution. What are they teaching you in that school of yours?"

Adam started to write his name. No, make that Anthony's name.

"Hey, mister, you never told me your name."

"Nick," the white-bearded gentleman replied. "Well, my real name is Nicolas. When I was young my mom used to call me Nicolas her little angel. I was a pretty precocious lad. I didn't like being called an angel, though. Thankfully, as I got older, she switched from calling me an angel to calling me a saint. It's hard living up to the standards of a saint, you know, but I do my best."

Saint Nicolas? What are the chances of a big-bellied guy with a huge white beard being called Saint Nick? Adam thought for a moment and then dismissed the ridiculous notion.

"So, Nick, do you live around here?"

"Nope. My wife and I are from up north. I'm just on a little vacation."

"Vacation? But you're working."

"Heck, this isn't work, son; it's fun. It isn't work when you do something that you like. That's what's wrong with people today. They aren't having enough fun. Ho, ho, ho, I'm having a grand old time helping people like you. It's a great job when you can make a person smile."

Ho, ho, ho? Who laughs like that? This is very weird, Adam thought. "What do you do up north?"

"I'm a deliveryman. It's seasonal work, mostly done at night."

A fat deliveryman, sporting a white beard, who lives up north, works at night, and goes by the name of Nick. St. Nick? Nah, it couldn't be! Adam thought. "You wouldn't by any chance own a few reindeer would you?"

Nick lifted his eyebrow slightly. "I couldn't own a reindeer any more than your mother could own you," he replied. "It wasn't God's intention for any of his creations to be owned. But I'll tell you one thing: if you treat a person or an animal with kindness and respect, they will do anything for you."

Adam didn't know what to say except for "yes, sir."

"Now let's work on this little problem of yours." Nick started entering data into a computer keyboard. "I'll just type in the cell number, and the computer will give me the ESN number. There it is: SAR-111555. It looks like someone's birth date to me. I guess that's just the silly way I look at things."

"Did you find the phone's location yet?" Adam asked.

"Oh heavens no, that will take some time. I'll call you when I get that information."

"Call me?"

"Why, certainly. How else would I notify you? By smoke signals?"

"You can't call me; I don't have a phone."

"I didn't mean that I would call you on a cell phone. I'll call your house."

"No, you can't do that!" Adam pleaded. "My mother will find out," he lied.

"Oh yes," he said, smiling. "We can't have that, now could we?"

"How about if I just wait here?"

"It may take a few hours. I'm sure a boy like you has something better to do with his time. Why don't you go outside and play with your friends?"

"I don't know where they are right now," Adam replied.

"Oh well, you know what they say: good friends are hard to find!"

"You sure got that right," Adam remarked.

"If you must wait, how about having some milk and cookies? There's nothing better than milk and cookies, wouldn't you agree? I especially love them when I'm doing my deliveries." Nick smiled. "Look at this belly of mine. It's because of the milk and cookies, you know."

"You're not so fat," Adam remarked.

"Fat? Who said anything about being fat? You know, there are many people obsessed with their weight. Can you guess what they become?"

"No," Adam answered.

"They become very unhealthy and unhappy skinny people who are hungry all the time."

Adam giggled. What Nick said was true.

"I hope you don't think that you have to look like one of those string beans to be popular. It's wrong to think that way, you know. Popularity has more to do with what you *do* than what you *eat*. Take me for example. I'm happy with who I am and what I am. If you ask me, I'm just the right size. I don't think that you could find one person in the entire world who dislikes me because of my big belly, and that's a fact!"

"Okay, okay, I'll have some cookies and milk. And I'm sorry I called you fat. I'll never say that word again, I swear."

Nick smiled and retired to the back room to prepare the mid-day snack.

Nobody is ever going to believe me when I tell them about this guy, Adam thought. *I don't even believe this myself! Should I ask him if he knows any elves? Nah, I don't want to find out that he does.*

Nick returned holding a silver tray on which was a large pitcher of milk and an enormous plate of homemade chocolate chip cookies that smelled incredible. They both sat and ate the cookies as if they were the best food on earth. Adam helped himself to two glasses of milk. For the first time since the fire, he was happy. Somehow Nick knew that, and it made him feel great.

It seemed like no time before the computer printed out the cell phone's location. Nick took the paper from the printer and handed it over.

"Here's a signal-strength coverage map. Your phone should be somewhere in this area." He pointed to the shaded area.

"This is great!" Adam replied. "It's the best present I ever got!"

Nick smiled and replied, "I know!"

CHAPTER TWENTY-FIVE

The fire marshal had just handed him the finished report. According to evidence collected at the scene, the fire at the Simmons' residence was caused by an incendiary device located in the basement. The device was triggered to explode by a small timer, which was found in the basement rubble. It was pure and simple; the fire was not accidental, it was intentionally set by an arsonist. The fact confirmed his original hypothesis.

While happy with the fire marshal's report, Detective Tim Faraday now had another crime to add to his collection. Arson, kidnapping, burglary, and reported gunshots simply did not exist in Huntingdon Valley. That was until the last week or so. Although he had no direct evidence pointing to Tony the Match, Faraday knew there had to be a connection. One of the counter people at Valley Burgers had described a man fitting Tony's description as the man who had thrown his breakfast tray to the ground and then ran out the front door just moments before the shooting in the alley behind the restaurant. Apparently, Tony the Match was after Anthony Trent, but why?

He remembered, from years ago, when he was a student at the police academy, the lectures on proven detective techniques. The basics were constantly stressed. "Who, what, where, and why—learn the answers to those questions and you'll solve any crime," his instructors had pointed out.

Faraday knew the what and the where, and he had a good idea

about the who, but he was at a dead end with the why. He looked at his notes taken during the first interrogation with Tony the Match. Though Tony had admitted to nothing at the time, there were some odd facts regarding his knowledge about Gina Nano and the demise of Adam Simmons. Tony had insinuated that Adam was alive.

Was that possible? Could Adam have survived the fire?

A witness at Valley Burgers stated that there had been two boys being shot at in the rear alley. If one of them was Anthony Trent, could the other have been Adam Simmons? If so, was he responsible for breaking into Anthony's bedroom? What was he looking for? What was Adam's Gameboy doing in Anthony's bedroom? The biggest piece of the puzzle was how Adam, if alive, was able to move about the neighborhood without being recognized. Was the kidnapper going after Adam's friends in the hope of catching Adam? There had to be an answer. Perhaps Tony the Match should be interrogated again.

...

"I'm flattered. It ain't often that someone likes me enough to see me twice," Tony stated.

"I guess I enjoy torturing myself," Faraday replied.

"Whatever turns you on, that's my motto."

"What turns you on, Tony?" Faraday asked.

"Well, it sure ain't being dragged in here and asked stupid questions."

"How about setting homes on fire? Does that turn you on?"

Tony curled his upper lip in anger.

"Look, cop, I don't know where you're going here, but if you don't cool it with those kinds of questions, I'll be happy to show you what fire is really about."

"I was just wondering why you were chasing after two boys behind Valley Burgers."

"Oh yeah, and who told ya that?"

"Witnesses, Tony. And in case you don't understand what that word means, I'll explain it to you very slowly. You were seen at Valley Burgers, you threw a tray of food on the floor; then you exited the front door, ran to the back alley, and started shooting at two boys, one of whom was Anthony Trent, and the other was Adam Simmons. Now, what do you have to say about that?"

"I'd say that you got a screw loose somewhere. Adams Simmons died in a fire. Ain't you heard that on TV?"

"That's what everyone thinks, but you know different, don't you, Tony?"

"I ain't seen nobody who looks like Adam Simmons. Have you, cop?"

"No, but that doesn't mean anything. He might be wearing a disguise."

"Yeah, and I might be Abraham Lincoln. Oh, I forgot, he's dead, too. Listen, cop, the last time I checked, it's not against the law to buy food at Valley Burgers. If I wanna throw it on the floor, that's my business."

"What about shooting at the boys, Tony?"

"What boys? I saw some rats behind the joint, and I shot at them. I was doin' a public service. Too bad they got away."

"Rats with two legs, Tony?"

"Rats is rats. I don't know nothin' about legs."

"Do you know it's against the law to fire a gun without a permit?"

"Imagine that, you guys have a rat killing law. Okay, it's your town. If you want me to leave the rats alone, I'll do it. I wouldn't want you to think that I'm some kinda criminal. If you want, I'll even donate some money to your favorite rat charity."

"That won't be necessary, but I would like your gun," Faraday insisted.

"My gun?" Tony attempted to search himself. "Oh yeah, I forgot, I lost it!"

"You lost it?"

"Yeah, ain't it a shame?"

"A shame, Tony, do you know what's a shame?"

"Nah, what?" Tony replied.

"It's a shame that you're not in jail. But don't worry, Tony; I'm working on that!"

CHAPTER TWENTY-SIX

Anthony was a very unhappy camper. He was tied to a chair, gagged, and blindfolded. He kept rocking the chair back and forth, causing it to bang against the wall, hoping the noise would be heard. Unfortunately, his efforts attracted the attention of the wrong person. He felt someone lift the blindfold off his eyes. It was the old man.

"Anthony, you're making too much noise. Don't you realize that your life is in danger? You don't want to be killed, do you, boy? Now I suggest you sit quietly, like your friend over there."

Anthony turned to the left and saw Gina sitting gagged and bound to a chair. She acknowledged him by shaking her head.

"I know that you must have many questions. If you promise not to yell, I'll temporarily remove the gag from your mouth."

Anthony shook his head up and down.

Once the gag was removed he asked quietly, "Why did you kidnap us?"

"That's a long story, which I currently have no time to tell. You will find out soon enough, though," the old man replied.

"Are we going to die?"

The old man laughed. "Sooner or later everybody dies. The question you should be asking is if you are going to die in the near future."

Anthony took a big gulp. "Are you going to kill us?"

The old man laughed again. "Now, do I look like a killer to you?"

"No, sir," Anthony stammered.

"Good," said the old man. "Do you have any more questions?"

Anthony was too afraid to ask any more questions. He shook his head no, and the old man replaced the gag in his mouth.

"I know that you and Gina are scared, but I assure you that as long as you are quiet you won't be harmed. I must leave you for now, but don't worry; it will only be for a short time. Perhaps I will be lucky enough to find Adam. I'm sure you both would like that very much. While you're sitting down here in the dark, I want you to remember one thing: you're safer with me than you are with Tony, the guy with the big nose. If you make any noise and Tony discovers this hiding location, you may not live to see tomorrow. Do you understand what I am saying?"

They both nodded their heads in agreement.

"Good." The old man smiled and walked up the stairs. He closed what appeared to be a wooden trapdoor. Anthony and Gina were alone, surrounded only by darkness and humming machinery.

Chapter Twenty-Seven

....

Adam removed the computer printout from his back pocket. He carefully unfolded it and spread it out on the bed in the room he was currently using as a hiding place in the basement of the Bryn Athyn Museum. According to the cellular signal-strength map, Anthony's mom's phone was located at one of three possible places: Gold's Funeral Home, the Merit gas station, or Aldo's Italian Café. Using logic, he quickly ruled out the gas station because, aside from two small bathrooms, there was only a glass-enclosed office, which certainly wasn't large enough to hide Anthony and Gina. Aldo's restaurant was a possibility, but he determined that the funeral home would have the most hiding places. He just hoped that his two friends weren't lying in a coffin in the dark recesses of the basement.

To draw the least amount of suspicion, he decided that the best approach would be to simply walk in the front door and ask questions, posing as a student interested in the daily operations of a funeral home. If he could get someone to show him around, perhaps he could spot some evidence that might lead him to his friends. He would take notes of all the exit doors and other possible ways he might use as an entrance later that night when they were closed.

Do funeral homes close at night? he wondered. *What happens if a person dies at 1:00 a.m.? My parents died at that hour. Did the funeral home wait until the morning?*

He found himself wiping tears from his eyes. The lump in his throat became impossible to swallow. The thought of never seeing his parents again was too much for him to bear. For the rest of his life, he would be on his own, with no one to help him. There would be no mother to tuck him into bed and no more soft kisses to his forehead when he got sick. There would be no father to cheer him on when he played baseball, roller hockey, or basketball. The worst part was that he would no longer have his mom or dad to hug when he needed one so desperately. It took a Herculean effort to push the sadness back inside his broken heart. Unfortunately, there was nothing he could do about his parents, but with some luck, he could save his friends. He held himself accountable for their disappearance and deemed it his responsibility to rescue them from harm's way.

He checked his disguise, which consisted of a realistic stick-on mustache, a wrap-around pair of Ambervision sunglasses, a geeky polo shirt, and a pair of white pants that he had appropriated from a mannequin he found in the basement. If he combed his hair with a part on the side, he could easily have been hired by Microsoft.

...

"Hello, how can I help you?" asked the impeccably dressed man with slicked-back hair. He was wearing a custom-tailored black suit, white starched shirt, and red silk tie.

"My name is Jay…," Adam tried to say without showing any nervousness, "Jay…ah…Roth. I am a new student, recently transferred to Huntingdon High, and I'm wondering if you could help me."

The man reached out to shake hands. "My name is Bruce Gold. Are you here to make arrangements?"

"Arrangements?" Adam asked.

The man invited Adam into the lobby of Gold's Funeral Home. "Normally, we discuss arrangements with someone older. Perhaps you would like to wait for your mother and father."

Tears appeared in the corners of Adam's eyes. "My mother and father are dead," he replied in a wavering voice.

"Oh dear, I'm sorry. How insensitive of me. You poor lad, it's just that we're not used to making arrangements with someone so young."

"I'm not so young," Adam quickly pointed out. He was somewhat disappointed. He thought that his disguise made him look at least sixteen.

Mr. Gold smiled. "I didn't mean to offend you, but you don't look much more than twenty-one."

Now Adam was smiling. "Yes, they are always asking my age when I go to bars."

"Perhaps we should retire to my office," Mr. Gold suggested.

They both walked down a long hall and entered a door that was marked private.

The office was decorated very tastefully. Mr. Gold took a seat behind a large walnut desk that was located in the center of the room. He beckoned to Adam to sit in the overstuffed chair in front of the desk. As Adam faced Mr. Gold, he could see a large painting of a sunset that hung on the wall behind the desk. There were no file cabinets, just a matching walnut credenza, which was within close proximity of the desk.

Mr. Gold started taking notes on a legal pad. He read aloud as he wrote. "Let's see, your name is Jay Roth." He looked at Adam for a moment. "Age twenty-one. Is that correct?"

"Yes, sir," Adam stammered.

"The address is?" Mr. Gold asked.

"Address for what?" Adam asked.

"For the pickup," Gold answered.

"The pickup?" Adam asked, expressing confusion.

"Yes, for the bodies," Mr. Gold replied.

"The bodies?" Adam asked.

"Yes, the bodies of the recently departed, your parents."

A sudden bout of sadness assaulted Adam. The lump once again grew in his throat, and tears formed in the corners of his eyes. Try as he might, he found it difficult to speak.

Mr. Gold came from behind the desk and put his arm around him for comfort.

"Son," he said, "there is no chore more difficult in life than dealing with the death of a loved one. While it is true that time heals all wounds, it is not so apparent at this particular moment. There is no shame in expressing your sadness for a loved one, whether it be today, tomorrow, or forever."

He offered Adam a tissue. "Don't worry," Mr. Gold said. "It's okay to cry. I have as many tissues as you have tears." For the first time since his parents died, Adam had someone to hug.

After a few moments, Mr. Gold suggested that they take a walk. Feeling somewhat better, Adam agreed. As they strolled the halls, Adam found the courage to continue his quest, the search for his best friends. As they passed various closed doors, he asked Mr. Gold to open them so he could see the behind-the-scenes operation. Mr. Gold was reluctant, but succumbed to Adam's relentless curiosity. All of the rooms were empty.

"We do most of our work in the lower level," Mr. Gold explained.

"Can we go there?" Adam asked.

"That is a most unusual request, son. I don't believe that it would be wise in your particular frame of mind."

Adam gave a slight smile. "It's something that I need to do. I can deal with it. Can't I see the basement...please?"

"Maybe just for a moment, but no longer," Mr. Gold replied.

They walked down the stairs located at the rear of the hall. As the stairwell echoed with each step, Adam's heart began to pound until it felt like it was going to escape his chest. Mr. Gold saw his distress and asked if they should continue.

"I'm just a little nervous," Adam replied.

Bruce Gold remembered the first time his father brought him to the lower level. He recalled being more than just a little nervous; he had been downright frightened. As they opened the door at the bottom of the stairwell and entered the basement hall, they immediately smelled a mixture of not-so-pleasant odors, ranging from bleach to various disinfecting chemicals. Adam looked a little green around the gills.

"Are you sure that you want to continue?" Mr. Gold asked.

Adam nodded his head. "I think I should visit the bathroom first."

Mr. Gold remembered telling his father the same thing. He pointed to a door no more than ten feet away. "The bathroom is right there. I'll wait outside until you are ready."

Adam entered the bathroom and turned the little latch on the door for privacy. He threw some cold water on his face, being careful not to dislodge his mustache. This was a lot tougher than he thought. He went over to the window and opened it to get some fresh air. The thought occurred to him that if he left the window lock unlatched, he could use the window to gain entrance later that night. After a few minutes of breathing fresh air, Adam closed the window and moved the latch just enough so it would appear to be locked. He flushed the toilet for effect, washed his hands, and left the bathroom with a slight smile on his face.

"I see you are feeling better," Mr. Gold remarked.

"Yes," Adam replied. "Going to the bathroom was a good idea."

As they walked the hall, Adam questioned Mr. Gold as to what was behind certain closed doors.

"Those are storage closets containing chemicals and various dry goods," Mr. Gold lectured. He pointed to a very large set of closed double doors. "That's cold storage."

"Cold storage?" Adam asked.

"Yes, the low temperature is required to maintain preservation."

Adam nodded his head as if he understood.

"The room to the right is used for preparation," Mr. Gold continued.

Preparation for what? Adam thought. "Can we go in that room?"

"Absolutely not," Mr. Gold stated. "We must abide by strict health regulations. Only a licensed mortician is allowed in that room."

Adam heard a noise coming from behind the closed door on the right.

"Who's in there?" he asked.

"That's the shomer," Mr. Gold replied.

"The shomer?" Adam asked.

"The shomer is like a religious watchman that stays with the deceased until burial," Mr. Gold replied.

A watchman? Adam thought. *Sounds like a guard to me. Maybe the shomer is guarding Anthony and Gina.*

Adam reached for the doorknob.

"Stop!" Mr. Gold commanded. "You can't go in there."

"Why not?" asked Adam.

"It's disrespectful. I know you may find this difficult to understand, but we follow certain traditions and guidelines. Respect for the deceased must always be maintained. Perhaps we should go back upstairs."

Adam followed Mr. Gold to the stairwell. He made mental notes of the rooms he needed to visit later on that evening. He hoped the shomer wasn't the big, ugly guy with the humongous nose.

"Perhaps we should discuss the arrangements now," Mr. Gold suggested. He opened the door to his office and motioned for Adam to go in.

"I'd like to come back later," Adam said—which, in this case, was not far from the truth.

"But what about your parents? This can't be postponed; arrangements must be made."

Adam smiled. "Don't worry, Mr. Gold. I'll come back. I promise."

He shook Bruce Gold's hand and left.

Chapter Twenty-Eight

While the residents slept, a big black Cadillac rolled slowly down the streets of Huntingdon Valley in search of prey. The hunt for Adam Simmons had become an obsession of Tony the Match's. A few days earlier, it had been just a job, but now it was personal. He was being ridiculed by his boss. And then there was that pesky detective, Tim Faraday, who had insinuated that he had a thing for setting houses on fire, which was wrong because he liked setting *everything* on fire. When he finally got Adam in his big burly hands, he would show Faraday what he really thought about fire.

With a full tank of gas and fresh batteries for his night scope, he took to the streets, once again scanning the neighborhood. Upon finding Adam and his friends, he would take pleasure in killing them and stuffing their bodies in one of those trash bins behind the high school. Then he'd set the bin on fire. Maybe to celebrate, he'd invite his boss and Faraday to a marshmallow roast. Wouldn't that be something?

...

Adam had spent the last hour preparing for the break-in at the funeral home. He wore black clothing and had covered his hands and face with dirt. In the darkness of night, he would be practically invisible. Staying off all the main streets, he pedaled Anthony's bike quickly until he reached the rear of the building. With only one parking lot light casting an eerie yellow glow against the black asphalt, he approached with caution.

He hid the bike in a nearby shadow and walked to the basement bathroom window that he had left unlocked. Being careful to make the least amount of noise possible, Adam pushed on the window until it opened and then climbed in. From the window to the bathroom floor was a drop of only five feet, but in the darkness it seemed much higher. He jumped and landed on the white ceramic tile with a thud.

Cupping his ear to the door, he stood quietly for a moment trying to hear any noise in the hallway. When he determined that it was safe, he gently inched the door open and peeked through the crack. A single flickering light overhead gave the hallway a sense of peril, which brought back memories of the movie *Raiders of the Lost Ark*. He imagined that he was Indiana Jones in search of untold treasure.

He left the confines of the bathroom and slowly crept through the hallway while hugging the wall. Upon reaching the first door on the right, he tried the knob; it was locked. He continued to the next door and found that it was locked as well. He remembered Mr. Gold mentioning that they were storage closets. Chances were that his friends wouldn't be locked in such small rooms.

His trek continued until he arrived in front of two large white doors with a sign that indicated cold storage. Although he thought it odd to keep a refrigerator in the basement, he was thirsty, and a nice cold soda would do the trick.

As he opened one of the doors, an interior light automatically came on. He quickly entered and closed the door behind him. The room was extremely cold and quite large for a refrigerator. To his dismay, there were no cases of soda or any other types of food lying about. Aside from a long metal cart and what appeared to be cabinets with stainless steel handles mounted on the far wall, the entire room was empty.

Thinking that the soda was stored in a cabinet, he decided to pull one of the stainless steel handles. A three-foot-square door opened.

Adam peeked inside and saw nothing but a movable shelf, which easily glided through the square opening. There were many doors; surely one of them contained the soda. He continued from door to door, peeking inside, none of them yielding any more than an empty movable shelf. He finally reached a cabinet door with a small sign indicating the contents within. Although he preferred a Coke, his second choice of soda matched the name on the door: Dr. P. Pepper.

He pulled on the handle, easily opening the door. Apparently, the Dr. Pepper had been placed on the moveable shelf under a large black tarp. With great difficulty, he attempted to pull the shelf through the small opening. It barely budged. The Dr. Pepper had to weigh over 200 pounds. He pulled with all his might, exerting more energy than he thought possible, which, in turn, fueled his thirst. He was so parched that he could drink a six-pack of the soda.

Just as he was about the lift the tarp, he heard a noise outside in the hall. He realized that a passerby might notice the light coming from under the door of the room he was in. He frantically searched for the light switch. He then realized what his father had once pointed out as a catch-22. He planned on hiding inside one of the cabinets, but if he turned out the light, the room would be too dark to find the cabinet.

The noise in the hall was just outside the door. There was no time to push the Dr. Pepper back into its resting place. Adam jumped onto a moveable shelf and pulled himself into the close confines of its corresponding cabinet. He didn't realize how claustrophobic it was to be, lying in such a small, dark space. He heard someone walk into the cold-storage room.

"Who left the light on?" the person asked. "And why is Dr. Pepper out?"

Adam heard a groan as the Dr. Pepper was pushed back into its cabinet. Then the room was thrown into blackness as the person turned off the light and left the room. Adam used his arms to propel the sliding shelf back out. Although the room was very cold, he found himself sweating profusely. He couldn't wait to escape the darkness of the cold-storage room. Fumbling in the darkness, he bumped his knee into the long metal cart that stood in the center of the room. Using great care, he edged his way along the outer walls until he found the light switch and flipped it back on. The fear of getting caught was stronger than his thirst. He opened the door and walked back into the hall and continued the search for his friends.

Something metallic hitting the floor caught his attention. The sound appeared to come from the far end of the hall. He crept along the wall until he reached a door that was cracked open just enough for him to peer inside. An old man was sitting on a chair in the corner, reading a book. He was wearing a white skull cap and a matching shawl. It had to be the shomer that Mr. Gold had mentioned earlier. Surely, this couldn't be the person who was guarding Anthony and Gina.

He thought for a moment. Maybe that's what they wanted him to think. Perhaps the man was not old at all. It could be the kidnapper wearing a disguise. Hidden underneath that shawl was a weapon, Adam was sure of it. He had to come up with some way of making the crazed, kidnapping shomer leave the room so he could search for his friends.

Racing back to the bathroom, he formulated a plan. His idea was to roll toilet paper into a wad large enough to overflow the toilet. Once the water began to flood, he would yell for help and then hide in the cold-storage area while the shomer dashed to the bathroom. During the time that it took for the shomer to unclog the toilet, Adam would rush back to where his friends were held and free them from danger. It was a simple yet effective strategy.

"Help! Help! The bathroom is flooding! The bathroom is flooding!" he yelled and then ducked into the cold-storage room.

Just as he had planned, the shomer came running. No, shuffling would be a better description. The old man was holding on to a metal walker as he slowly pushed it toward the bathroom. Upon reaching the flood, the old man murmured something that sounded like "Oy vey. Vas ist das?"

Adam took the opportunity to dart back to the room the old man had come from. His heart raced as he flung the door open and ran inside. The room was a lot smaller than he had thought. It contained very little furniture and no closets, just a chair and what appeared to be a bed. Because of the drawn covers, Adam couldn't make out who was sleeping in the bed.

Maybe the kidnappers had tied Anthony and Gina, thrown them on the bed, and covered them so they wouldn't accidentally be seen. Well, Adam was too smart to fall for that trick. He moved to the bed and ripped the covers away. What he saw would be difficult to ever forget. It certainly wasn't one of his friends.

"Yikes!" he screamed.

"Vat in God's name ist going on here?"

Adam spun around and saw the old man standing in the doorway.

"Please don't kill me!"

"Vat are you, sum kind of qvazy person?"

Adam wondered what a qvazy person was. "A qvazy person?"

"Yah," the man answered. "A mashugana. A vild maniac. A cuckoo nincompoop! Vye you here?"

"I...I..." Adam couldn't speak.

"You must leaf!"—the shomer pointed to the door—"Und be qviet! GO!"

Adam started to run. He kept running until he was in the safety of the parking lot.

...

Tony the Match maneuvered his Cadillac onto Hunting Pike. It was three in the morning, and his stomach was making more noise than Craig Kartin, the late-night radio personality. Craig was shouting something about how the Philadelphia Eagles should draft new fans instead of players, and Tony was thinking about why Valley Burgers was closed.

Out of the corner of his eye he caught some motion. It was too dark to make out the details, but it looked like someone on a bike leaving the parking lot of Gold's Funeral Home. Tony grabbed the night scope from the passenger seat and held it to his eyes. Through the bright green haze, he could see the rider of the bike. Tony smiled as he threw the scope back unto the seat. The hunter had just found his prey.

CHAPTER TWENTY-NINE

Detective Tim Faraday had been tailing Tony the Match for hours. To not arouse suspicion, Tim had used his personal car instead of one of the department's black-and-white Crown Vics. The street traffic was sparse, and it was difficult to use the standard "four cars behind" tail that was taught by the police academy's driving instructor. Sometimes he wondered whether anything he learned at the academy could be applied in real-life situations. Regardless of what he had been taught, Tim found that common sense always offered the best solution. For the last two hours, he had been successfully following Tony's Cadillac by driving without the use of his headlights.

When Tony stopped in front of Gold's Funeral Home, it took Tim by surprise. Tim quickly pulled his car into the shadows of one of the big oak trees that lined Hunting Pike. It took a moment before he realized what Tony was doing. The two green glowing circles bouncing off of Tony's windshield could only be caused by the reflection of a night scope. The use of high-tech equipment proved that Tony was not as stupid as he appeared to be. What was it that caught Tony's interest?

The answer came whizzing by as a boy riding a bike nearly crashed into Tim's parked car. Before Tim could react, he saw Tony the Match in hot pursuit.

"What the heck is going on?"

Tim made a quick U-turn and followed Tony's big black monster of a car. It wasn't long before he saw Tony making a right on Fetter's

Mill Lane. Fetter's Mill Lane was barely a two-lane street, which made it difficult to drive in the darkness. Tim's common sense said it wouldn't be safe to follow in secrecy. Throwing caution to the wind, Tim proceeded without the use of his headlights.

A hundred yards down Fetter's Mill Lane, Tony's Cadillac stopped in front of the Bryn Athyn Museum. Tim decided it was best to park his car and continue on foot. He used the oak trees as cover as he cautiously moved closer to the museum. Within minutes he was standing behind a tree just across from the big black car. Tony was sitting in the driver's seat, once again using his night scope. It was difficult for Tim to see what held Tony's interest. As Tim's eyes grew accustomed to the darkness, he could make out the image of a boy entering the side door of the building. Tim watched as Tony left the car and followed the boy's path to the door. Tim carefully and quietly pursued.

...

Adam thought he was about to die. His clothes were damp from the sweat that came from every pore of his body. His heart was pounding like a freight train. What had been a mission to free his friends had become the scariest thing he had ever experienced. He would have nightmares for the rest of his life!

On the way back to his hidden lair at the museum, Adam could think of nothing except what he had seen at the funeral home. His mind kept replaying the image of what lay under the sheet. He was expecting to see Anthony or Gina, not a dead guy with bulging eyes! And then there was the old man yelling at him, calling him a mashugana. Whatever that meant, Adam was sure it was not a good thing. To top it off, he had smashed into a car and scratched Anthony's bike. If it weren't for bad luck, Adam would have no luck at all. He was exhausted, and all he wanted to do was go to sleep.

He hid the bike behind some of the museum's overgrown

landscaping bushes and used the side-entrance fire door that led to the basement stairwell. He had been sleeping in the basement for close to a week and knew that soon his luck would run out. The maintenance man was bound to find his hiding place in the near future, but for now, Adam wasn't worried about himself; he was worried about his friends. Were they dead or alive? If they were dead, would he have to make another midnight visit to the funeral home? He slapped his head. *Duh! The kidnapper wouldn't spend money on two coffins; he would just throw the bodies in a big hole and bury them. Nah, that would be too much work. It would be easier to throw the bodies into the Delaware River.* Adam pictured Gina and Anthony floating down the river, with their eyes bulging. It was a nightmare in the making.

He couldn't believe that his friends could be dead. It just wasn't possible. But then again, his parents were dead, and that didn't seem possible either. It took a great effort to have faith that his friends were still alive. But where were they? He looked at the cellular coverage map. If he ruled out the Merit gas station and Gold's Funeral Home, the only place left was Aldo's Italian Café. *Now where could they hide there?* Adam shuddered at the thought of opening the restaurant's freezer and finding his two friends, frozen, with bulging eyes, hanging on a meat hook. His mind was really coming up with some weird ideas. The image of bulging eyes was beginning to drive him crazy.

He walked down the deserted hall to the room he used as a hideout. He thought he heard a noise coming from the basement stairwell. *It must be a ghost with bulging eyes,* he thought. He nervously laughed to himself. *That's all I need. First, my parents die in a mysterious explosion; then my best friends get kidnapped, and now a ghost with bulging eyes. What else could happen to me?*

There was no sound coming from the basement stairwell; it was just his imagination getting the best of him; he was sure of it. He entered his secret lair, took off his clothes, climbed in bed, and pulled the covers over his head.

...

Tony was quite pleased with himself because soon Adam would be in his grasp. *Once I snatch the kid and bring him to the boss, it will prove that I ain't no dummy,* he thought. He walked down the stairwell until he reached the basement fire door, opened it, and entered the darkened hall. "Whatcha' doin', kid? Playing hide-and-seek?" he asked softly. "Well, I'm good at that game."

He remembered the time he played hide-and-seek with this friend, Dino Bigoni. He was ten years old at the time. They had been playing in the old, abandoned house on Pickering Lane. Dino had been the kind of kid that could get on your nerves. He thought he was the best at everything—the best soccer player, the best basketball player, the best baseball player. Whenever Dino had a bad day, he would blame it on his asthma. He carried around this little inhaler that he pulled out whenever he was losing at sports. He would sniff it and say, "I woulda won if it wasn't for my asthma." Sometimes Tony had wanted to shove that inhaler so far up Dino's nose that he would've needed a brain surgeon to get it out.

Dino had been hiding real good, too good. After twenty minutes of searching, Tony had decided that there was a better way of finding his friend. He had a great idea. Using the lighter that he had stolen from his mom, he went down to the basement and set the house on fire. The old house had smoked up pretty good before he heard his friend coughing in one of the bedrooms.

Tony had laughed. "I bet that inhaler ain't working so good."

He had dashed outside and waited for Dino to run into his arms, but that had never happened. Tony had watched as the house became one big fireball.

With another laugh, he had yelled to the flames, "You win, Dino! YOU WIN!"

Now Tony slowly walked down the hall, checking all the spots a kid might hide. "Come out, come out, wherever you are," he whispered. He opened door after door: no kid in sight. "Yo, kid, you sure you really want to play this game?" he continued as his hand reached for the lighter in his pocket. "How long do you think you can be quiet when this basement fills with smoke? Did you ever hear of asthma, kid? Do you got one of them inhalers? Are you gonna cough as loud as my old buddy Dino?" Tony pulled the lighter from his pocket. It was an old metal Zippo, the same lighter that he stole from his mom. Using his thumb, he flipped open the lid. "You wanna hear somethin' neat, kid?" He jerked his wrist, and the lid of the lighter snapped shut. Over and over again, he used his thumb to flip open the lid and then jerked his wrist to snap it shut. Click, click, click, click, the sound echoed in the empty hall. "You can only make that sound with a Zippo, kid." Leaving the lid open, he brought the lighter to his nose and sniffed. As he drew the fumes into his nostrils, he said, "Nothin' smells as good as a Zippo. It ain't like them cheap butane lighters, no sir. This here uses liquid lighter fuel. I bet you don't know what that is, do ya, boy? Well, you're gonna find out soon, real soon."

One of the rooms that Tony had checked was not empty. With a big smile on his face, he entered. Finding exactly what he needed, his mind began to plan his devious scheme. The tiny room contained bundles of cardboard boxes that had been collapsed, folded, and tied with twine. There were also small stacks of newspapers similarly prepared for recycling. In the corner was a large metal drum half filled with empty soda cans, glass bottles, and used plastic containers.

Tony used his pocketknife to snip the twine of one of the cardboard box bundles. Then he cut the boxes into strips and placed them into the metal drum. Next, he took some of the newspapers, crumpled them into wads, and placed them in the drum, as well. It was perfect. The combination of newspapers, cardboard boxes, and plastic containers would smoke up real good. He dragged his newly created smoke-making drum out of the room and into the basement hall.

"Last chance, kid," he said. "Come out, come out, wherever you are!"

Tony withdrew the Zippo from his pocket and flipped open the lid. He drew his thumb across the flint wheel and quickly turned it to make a spark. Instantly, a yellow-and-blue flame appeared. Tony's smile grew wider as he was about to light the newspaper lying across the top of the drum.

Suddenly, the lights in the basement hall went out.

"What the hell?" he shouted. "What's goin' on?"

He heard a noise behind him, but before he could react he felt something hard smack him on the back of his head. The lighter fell out of his hand as he slumped over the drum and lost consciousness.

Detective Tim Faraday was in the stairwell when the lights went out. Using his mini flashlight, he carefully walked the remainder of the stairs until he reached the basement fire door. Before opening it, he made sure that the bullets were chambered in his gun and the safety was off. Crouching low, he kicked open the door. The hall was dark except for the pencil-thin beam that came from his flashlight. In the middle of the hall, he spotted what appeared to be Tony hugging a big metal drum. With his gun in one hand and flashlight in the other, he cautiously approached.

"Friend of yours?" a voice asked.

Tim probed the darkness with the flashlight to discover the person behind the voice. A notably short, scrawny fellow wearing a pointy hat and red overalls was holding a metal pipe in his hands.

"Looking for me?" he asked.

"Who are you?" asked Tim.

"My name is Svensen, but my friends call me Trix. And who might you be?"

"I'm Police Detective Faraday, but my friends call me Tim. If you want to be my friend, I suggest that you put down that pipe. Okay, Trix?"

Trix lowered the pipe and extended his hand. "Glad to meet you, Tim."

After the handshaking formalities, Trix asked if it was okay to turn on the lights. With Tim's approval, the fluorescent ceiling tubes flickered back on.

In the lit room, Tim could see that Tony was not hugging the drum, he was slumped over it. "What happened here?" he asked.

"Found this guy in the hall about to set this drum on fire," Trix replied. "I accidentally hit him on the back of his head with this pipe."

"You accidentally hit him?"

"Sure. You don't think I would do something like that on purpose, do you?"

Tim looked at Tony's lifeless body and said, "No. In fact, I've been thinking about accidentally hitting him myself."

"No kidding? So I'm not in trouble?" Trix asked.

Tim reached out to shake Trix's hand once again. "No, you're not in trouble. In fact, I want to thank you."

"Can I ask you something, Tim?"

"Sure."

"Why did this guy want to set the place on fire?"

"That's a good question, Trix. I guess we'll find that out after he wakes up."

"What should we do with him until then?" Trix asked.

"I guess I should handcuff him and carry him to my car. I might need a hand. He looks a little heavy."

"No problem," Trix replied. He walked over to Tony and lifted him effortlessly over his shoulders.

Tim couldn't believe his eyes. Tony's body was twice that of Trix's height and weight, yet the little guy seemed to be holding him with no problem.

"What are you, a weightlifter or something?" Tim asked.

"Not really. I'm a toymaker by trade. I'm just working here part-time."

"A toymaker? I never met a toymaker before. Do you work for Mattel?"

"No, I work for a guy named Nick from up north. He and I came down here for a little rest and relaxation. He got a job at a cell phone store, and I got this job as a maintenance man. This is a nice little town you have here, Detective Tim."

"It'll be a lot nicer once we get rid of the trash," Tim replied. "Do you need a hand there?"

"Heck no. Bags of toys are much heavier than this."

Tim watched as the little guy carried Tony up the stairs and placed him in the car.

"Can I ask you a question, Trix?"

"Sure."

"Have you seen a boy around here?"

"I can't say that I have," Trix replied. "Now can I ask you a question, Tim?"

Tim nodded his head.

"Has the boy been naughty or nice?" Trix asked.

"I don't think the boy that I am looking for is a bad kid, if that's what you mean," Tim replied

Trix had a pixie-like smile on his face. "In my business, being good can make all the difference. Well, it was nice to meet you, Tim. And if you see Nick, tell him I said hello."

Tim was very confused. "I don't know what Nick looks like."

Trix kept the silly grin on his face and said, "You'll know him when you see him!"

CHAPTER THIRTY

Adam spent the whole night tossing and turning in bed. His dreams replayed images of his father pushing him out the window, his house blowing up, Ginger eating his father's note, being shot at by a big guy with a humongous nose, his friends disappearing, and a dead man with bulging eyes. To top it all off, he could have sworn he heard the voice of some guy who wanted to play hide-and-seek. By morning, Adam couldn't wait to wake up.

He shook the cobwebs from his brain and began to plan his day. When would be the best time to go to Aldo's restaurant? What would he do once he was there? Should he just walk in as a customer and say, "Let me have a slice of pizza, a Coke, and my two friends Anthony and Gina"? "Sure, that would work," he mumbled to himself.

He changed his clothes and put his ear to the door. Thankfully, it was quiet, which indicated that the maintenance man was somewhere else. He walked out into the basement hallway. Everything seemed normal except for a big metal drum at the far end of the hall. *That wasn't here last night,* he thought. As he approached the drum, he could see some clothing that had been folded neatly and placed on the floor. *Why would someone leave their clothes here?*

He picked up the clothes hoping he could find the identification of the owner. It was the strangest wardrobe he had ever seen. In his hands was a pair of red overalls that would fit a person no bigger than four feet tall. Matching the overalls was a pointed red hat with white trim. But the weirdest part of the outfit was a little pair of pointed red sneakers that might fit someone with tiny feet. The outfit looked vaguely familiar, but Adam couldn't quite remember where he had seen it before.

. . .

"Wake up, sleepyhead!" Tim shouted.

Tony groaned and opened one of his eyes. "What's goin' on? Where am I?"

"Welcome to my world, you ugly excuse for a human being," Tim replied.

"Your world?"

"Yes, my world. You're sitting in my office, wearing my handcuffs, and—oh, I forgot—you're under arrest!"

"Under arrest? For what?"

"For improper use of recyclables."

"Hey, man, I have a headache, and I don't know what you're talking about," Tony growled.

"Let me refresh your memory. You illegally entered the Bryn Athyn Museum, broke into a recyclable storage room, pulled a drum filled with newspaper and cardboard out into the hallway, and attempted to set it on fire."

"No kiddin'? Who told ya that?"

"I have the testimony of a witness."

"A witness? I don't believe you. In fact, I'm the victim here. Some big jerk slugged me in the back of my head with somethin'. So if you got a witness, I want him arrested for—what do you call it? Oh yeah—assault and battery!"

Tim laughed. "You weren't snookered by a big jerk. And for your information, he was a very nice fellow. He said you accidentally fell backward into the pipe that he was holding."

"And you believe that story? That's the biggest bunch of crap I ever heard."

Tim started to laugh. "Of course I believe the witness's story. Why would a four-foot midget lie to me?"

"A four-foot midget? I was slugged by a four-foot midget? Now I know you're lying!"

"Well, to tell you the truth, you might have a point there. He might not have been four feet tall. Come to think of it, he might have been a little shorter, but it was dark, and I didn't have a tape measure with me."

"Listen, cop, don't you think your story about a midget is a little weak?"

"No, I don't. As a matter of fact, nothing about this midget is weak. He's the one who carried you on his shoulders up the stairs and then put you in my car!"

"Now I know you're nuts!" shouted Tony. "I wanna call my lawyer."

"There's plenty of time for that, but for now, why don't we just have a cup of coffee and a friendly little chat?"

"How am I gonna do that with these handcuffs on?"

"If you promise to be nice and not set my office on fire, I'll take off the cuffs."

"Sure, whatever," growled Tony with a look that could kill.

Tim thought for a moment and smiled. "On second thought, maybe a cup of caffeine is a bad idea. We'll keep the cuffs on until you calm down, which in your case may be forever."

"You can't do that!" Tony screamed. "I got rights!"

Tim took a moment to pour himself a cup of black coffee. "Oh really? I am not aware of any law that gives you the right to a cup of coffee."

"You know what I mean, cop. You can't keep me in these cuffs forever, and you gotta let me talk to a lawyer!"

Tim slowly sipped his coffee while ignoring Tony's last outburst.

"Are you listening to me, cop?"

CHAPTER THIRTY-ONE

As the trapdoor opened, a stream of light slowly began to work its way across the basement floor, gently nudging the sleepy bodies of Anthony and Gina.

"Good morning," the old man said in a cheerful voice. "How was your sleep?"

The two gagged and groggy children could only nod their heads.

"If you two promise to keep quiet, I will remove those gags."

Again they nodded. Immediately after the gags were removed, they both asked for water.

"Water? Don't you want something better than that?"

The old man showed them the two glasses of orange juice he was hiding behind his back. Because their hands were tied, he gently held the glasses to their lips.

"Drink it slowly," he warned. "In about an hour I'll bring you some breakfast. How does that sound?"

"Letting us go would sound a lot better," Anthony said quietly.

The old man smiled. "Don't worry. Today might be the day."

Gina's eyes grew wider. "You're going to let us go today?"

"Let's just say that things are looking pretty good," he replied. "Perhaps we might be seeing Adam. Wouldn't that be great?"

"What are you going to do to Adam?" Anthony asked.

"That's a surprise," the old man replied, "but for now you two are going to sit here and be quiet. Do you understand?"

They both pleaded with him, but to no avail; he replaced their gags. In his best Arnold Schwarzenegger impression he said, "I'll be back!"

He walked up the wooden steps through the opening and gently lowered the trapdoor. Not a sound came from the darkened room below.

The old man was quite pleased with all he had achieved. The abduction of Anthony and Gina had gone much better than he had expected. Tony was currently in custody, and he was expecting Adam to walk right into his lair. It was a good day indeed. He couldn't wait to have his little dinner meeting with the boss.

...

Adam tried to think of the best way to search for his friends at Aldo's restaurant. He remembered seeing a help wanted sign in the window. Perhaps he could apply for a job. Of course, the only experience he had was washing cars at the car wash. *Washing cars and washing dishes are pretty much the same thing,* he thought. *How hard can it be?*

Armed with a ton of self-confidence, he glued on his mustache, retrieved Anthony's bike from behind the bushes, and proceeded to the restaurant. Because it was daylight, he took the more scenic route through the woods.

Everything was going well until the front bike tire slipped on some wet leaves. He jammed on his brakes, but it was too late. He barely had time to jump off before the bike hit a tree and crumpled to the ground. The bike was damaged beyond repair. The front tire was bent, and half the spokes were broken. *Holy cripes! Anthony is going to kill me for ruining his bike.* He thought for a moment. *Maybe he'll be so happy when I rescue him that he won't even ask about his bike.*

He brushed off his clothes, checked his mustache, and continued his trek to the restaurant on foot.

...

"What took you so long?" Tony screamed at the lawyer. He rose out of the chair in anger. "I want out, and I want out NOW!"

"May I first propose that you calm down and talk in a civilized manner," suggested the gray-haired gentleman wearing a blue pin-striped Armani suit.

"Are you sayin' I ain't civilized? Because, if that's what you're sayin', I can show you how civilized my fists are!"

"Resorting to violence will only exacerbate the situation. It is apparent that you require my assistance. However, if you continue this little tirade of yours, I will leave."

Although Tony did not understand what *exacerbate* or *tirade* meant, he did understand the word *leave*. He sat back in the chair and did his best to calm down.

"That's better," his lawyer said. "Now then, after reviewing the particulars of your arrest and subsequent incarceration, I have concluded that the evidence was circumstantial at best. Although Detective Faraday has protested vehemently, I have persuaded the district attorney in the matter of your discharge."

Tony looked at the lawyer as if he came from another planet. "Hey, geek cut your fancy bull and tell me in English!"

The lawyer smiled and said, "I got you released."

Tony jumped up and, with a punch to the man's shoulder, shouted, "You're the man!"

Wincing in pain, the silver-haired lawyer stated, "Oh, I forgot, the boss wants to see you."

"He does? Where and when?"

"Aldo's restaurant. Now!"

CHAPTER THIRTY-TWO

The late-afternoon sun elongated the shadow that befriended Adam as he walked to the restaurant. During the final three blocks, Adam's mood had changed from confidence to despair. After checking the cellular coverage map that indicated the location of Anthony's mom's cell phone, he asked himself, *What if the map is wrong? And if it is right, it may not mean anything. Anthony and Gina may not be with the cell phone. They might be dead...just like my parents.* Pushing back his tears, he approached Aldo's. It looked safe enough. There were no cars in the parking lot. That, at least, was a good sign. He opened the door and entered.

Immediately, he was greeted by Ashley, the tap-dancing waitress, who did one of her fancier steps before showing him to a booth.

"Would you like a menu?" she asked.

"Nah, just a Coke." His mouth was so dry he could barely talk.

"No problemo," she replied, disappeared into the kitchen, then returned a minute later with his drink. "If you need anything else, just scream."

Screaming was exactly what Adam wanted to do, but instead he gulped down his Coke. A minute or two elapsed before he got up the courage to do some exploring. He walked to the kitchen door and peered through its diamond-shaped window. The kitchen was spotless and appeared to be empty.

Pushing the door open slightly, he said, "Hello, is anybody there?"

All that replied was the noise of the refrigerator motors.

Again he asked in a louder voice, "HELLO?"

In fear, the hair began to rise on his arms. There was someone behind him; he knew it. His knees began to tremble, and sweat poured from his forehead. Suddenly, he felt a hand on his shoulder.

"Looking for someone?" a voice from behind asked.

Adam spun around expecting to have a gun aimed at his chest. He tried to talk but could only say, "Uh…uh."

A short man of Asian descent found Adam's utterance very amusing and replied, "A teenager with nothing to say, how refreshing! A perfect example of the phrase "Silence is golden." You look somewhat ill. Perhaps it would be better if you sat down."

Adam looked terrible, and he felt faint. All the blood had drained from his face, giving it a ghostly appearance. His legs could barely support his body. With the man's help, he managed to get to a booth before collapsing.

"What is your name, son?"

"Ad…," Adam started to say, but then realized he couldn't use his real name. "Jay…Roth," he finally managed, after remembering the name he gave to Bruce Gold from the funeral home.

The man winked. "Jay? Hmmmm. There was a guy named Jay who used to come here all the time. I think he moved to Florida. He was a big guy who was pretty good with a basketball. I believe he was some kind of doctor. He liked being called Dr. J. Oh, I forgot. My name is Aldo Siclione."

"Aldo?" Adam asked. "You're the owner of the restaurant?" *There's no way this guy is Italian,* he thought.

"No, actually the bank is the owner. That is until I finish paying off the loan," replied Aldo. "Confucius say, 'You can't judge a restaurant owner by what he look like.'"

Adam shook his head. "That's not what he said. He said, 'You can't judge a book by its cover'!"

Aldo smiled. "Same thing!"

They both laughed.

"You're funny," said Adam. "I can't remember the last time I laughed like that."

"Either you have a short memory or a very sad life," Aldo pointed out.

He could see the change in the boy's face. It was apparent that a short memory was not his problem. He decided to change the subject.

"When was the last time you ate?"

"Yesterday," replied Adam.

"Stomach does not care what you ate yesterday, only interested in today. Make stomach happy, the rest of body smile!"

With that said, Aldo quickly disappeared into the kitchen and returned with two slices of pizza.

"This pizza is good," Adam said while shoving a slice into his mouth.

"Of course it's good. What purpose is it to make bad pizza? Bad pizza is like bad friends: can't get rid of fast enough!"

Adam laughed and asked, "What saying do you have about good pizza?"

Aldo thought for a moment and replied, "Good pizza like good friends: always want more!"

Without thinking, Adam said, "I don't care about more friends; I just care about the ones I have now."

"Are your friends in trouble?"

"Yes, and I don't know how to help them. I don't even know where they are!"

"Ah…good friends are hard to find!"

"You're the second person that has told me that."

"Wise people often think alike."

"I wish I was wise enough to know what to do," stated Adam.

"A wise man once said, 'The search for an answer does not always follow a straight path,'" Aldo lectured. "Sometimes you need a guide or mentor."

"A mentor?"

"Yes, someone to help you, an adviser or counselor."

A tear formed in Adam's eye. *What I really need is my parents!* he thought.

Aldo, recognizing the boy's distress, changed the subject. "Would you like to see the kitchen?"

Casually wiping the tear with the back of his hand, Adam answered, "Sure."

Aldo proudly showed off his domain. The kitchen was spotless. Pots and pans of every size hung from stainless steel hooks that were suspended from the white ceiling. The ovens and grills shone like silver mirrors. Even the white ceramic tiles on the walls glowed. But it was not the cleanliness that impressed Adam; it was the wonderful mixture of smells like roasted garlic, sautéed onions, and freshly baked bread. An old lady stood in the corner adding ingredients to a huge vat of sauce. She gave Adam a big smile. He couldn't help but smile in return.

"So, what do you think of my kitchen?" Aldo asked.

"This is the neatest kitchen I have ever seen," Adam replied.

"If you think this is neat, you have to see the basement."

"The basement?" Adam asked.

"Yes, the basement. That's where we store all the dry and canned goods. Besides all the refrigerators and soda machine pumps, there are at least 300 cans of tomatoes down there. You'd be surprised at what you might find below."

"Can I see it?"

"Sure," Aldo replied. He went to the double sink and pointed to a wooden panel underneath. "The basement is under this wooden door." Then he lifted the door, revealing a set of wooden steps.

As Adam approached the opening, Aldo said, "Be careful; you have to bend your head on the way down the steps. It's a little dark down there, but don't worry; I'll be right behind you."

Adam walked down the steps and noted the overhanging beam that jutted from the ceiling. Then he realized why he had to duck his head.

The light was dim, just as Aldo had predicted. As he reached the floor of the basement, he heard a loud sound above him. The wooden door had been slammed shut. All the light, which had come from above, had been extinguished. Adam was trapped in the dark.

CHAPTER THIRTY-THREE

Aldo greeted the boss as he entered the restaurant. "How nice to see you again, sir. I believe you have a reservation."

The boss was once again impeccably dressed. He wore a custom-tailored brown suit with a tan shirt and a beautifully matched silk tie. "I'm expecting to meet some people here. You don't mind that I came a bit early, do you?"

"Not at all, sir. The early bird gets the worm, but in your case, I'll bring you some freshly made breadsticks."

Aldo directed the boss to a large booth in the corner. "I hope you'll find this booth to your satisfaction. Would you like some homemade wine? My father brought it with him from the old country."

"Would that be Italy or China?" the boss asked.

"What do you think?" Aldo asked.

The boss thought for a moment. "I think it wouldn't matter if it's good."

Aldo smiled and walked to the kitchen.

The boss was talking on his cell phone when Aldo returned with two glasses of wine. He motioned Aldo to place the wine on the table and then waved him away.

"So, did you have any problems securing his release?" he said into the phone.

He listened to the response and then continued, "Tony has gone a little too far. I think it's time to show him who's the boss around here. He can't go around setting places on fire, at least not without my permission. I should have known that he couldn't be trusted. I should have listened to the old man, that new accountant of mine. Now, he's someone I can trust."

To the boss's surprise, his new accountant suddenly appeared in the dining room. He quickly disconnected his call and directed the old man to take a seat next to him. "What are you doing here?"

"I came here for the early-bird special. You get a full-course dinner for seven ninety-five. That's a five-dollar discount. Let me get out my little calculator, and I'll show you the result of that savings."

He spent a half minute inputting numbers.

"If you invest five dollars a week for fifty-two weeks for twenty years at a compounded interest rate of six percent, you will have over $10,971.96!"

After using the calculator again, he continued, "By my eating here twice a week, that would increase my investment 200 percent, which, by my calculations, when compounded, would add $21,943.93 to my retirement."

"You say you could make over 21K by eating at this restaurant?"

"That's right!"

"That's incredible. I bet you could show me all the things that I'm doing wrong."

A broad smile crept across the old man's face. "That's my plan, sir."

"You said something about your retirement?" asked the boss. "You're an old man. You may not be alive in twenty years."

The accountant winked. "I'm not as old as you might think. Might I ask, have you done any retirement planning?"

"I can't say that I have."

"With your permission, I can help plan the next twenty years of your life."

"I like the way you think." The boss patted the old man on the back and replied, "My life is in your hands."

"I was hoping you would say that." Looking at his watch, the accountant said, "I just realized that I must do something before dinner. Aldo requires my assistance on a little project that we've been working on. Please excuse me."

The boss picked up his wine glass and downed its contents with one gulp, then nodded his head, signaling his approval for the old man to leave.

...

When Tony entered he was in a sour mood. His Cadillac had been temporarily impounded by the police, and he was forced to take a taxi to the restaurant. His head ached from being hit by a midget, he had lost his favorite Zippo lighter, and now, to make matters worse, he had to face the boss.

Ashley, the tap-dancing waitress, greeted him at the door. Seeing Tony's misery put her in a very perky mood.

"Welcome to Aldo's. It's so nice to see you again," she announced sarcastically.

Tony answered with a growl. Ignoring his response, she followed him to the booth where the boss was sitting.

"Can I get you some water?" she asked.

Tony remembered the last time she had brought him water, and passed on the idea.

"Do you think you can manage to bring me wine without spilling it all over my suit?"

Before she could answer, the boss chimed in: "I took the liberty of ordering your wine." He moved the glass toward Tony.

Ashley was slightly disappointed. She had looked forward to seeing the effect of red wine on a blue suit.

"I'll bring you some fresh breadsticks and a nice hot bowl of red sauce," she said with a gleam in her eye. Then she tap danced away.

"Boy, am I hungry," Tony stated.

"You're hungry? That's all you have to say?"

Tony tried not to look at the boss. "Yeah, boss, I haven't eaten for a while."

The boss slammed his fist on the table.

"You haven't used your brain for a while either!"

Tony quickly finished his wine and desperately needed another glass, but Ashley was nowhere in sight.

"Boss, I ain't stupid."

"You're right. You're not stupid—you're an imbecile! An earthworm has more brains than you!"

"But boss—"

"Did I not tell you to be discreet? This is a small town. Everybody knows everybody's business. And you try to burn a museum down? Two fires in less than a month. Do you think that would seem a little suspicious?"

"But I wasn't tryin' to burn the place down," Tony pleaded.

"Oh, I see. You were hungry and just wanted to roast some marshmallows. Is that your explanation?"

"No, boss. I was tryin' to scare the kid."

"From the way I see it, you were attempting to bake the kid."

"Nah, boss, it wasn't like that at all. He was hiding, and I was tryin' to smoke him out. Then I got hit on the noggin by a midget."

The boss grabbed Tony by the tie and yanked as hard as he could.

"Evidently, this mysterious midget didn't hit you hard enough!"

Tony's face turned beet red. He had heard enough. He no longer cared about anything other than taking his fist and ramming it into his boss's face. He was just waiting for the boss to let go of his tie. Lucky for everyone's sake, Ashley appeared with the breadsticks and sauce.

"Be careful, they're hot!" she warned.

Suddenly, feeding his face became more important than rearranging the boss's nose. Tony grabbed a breadstick in each hand and shoved them in his mouth.

"You should dip them in this sauce," Ashley remarked as she placed the bowl on the table.

Her wish came true when Tony tried the sauce and managed to drip some on his pants. He looked down and groaned as the hot sauce proceeded to make a red stain as it burned his leg.

"And the sauce is hot also," she said with a giggle. "I'll get you some more wine."

The boss looked at Tony as he stuffed his face. *This man is not just an idiot, he's also a pig,* he thought. He picked up a breadstick, dipped it in the sauce, and tried to show Tony how a human being eats. It made no difference. Tony continued to devour the breadsticks until they were gone.

"They ain't bad wit the sauce," Tony stated and then belched. He yelled to the kitchen, "Yo, broad, bring us more of dem sticks. And don't forget da sauce!"

Hearing Tony's scream, the little old lady in the kitchen carefully ladled some of her secret red sauce in a large bowl and directed Ashley to deliver it to the men.

"I hope they don't fill up on breadsticks. Ashley, be a dear and tell Tony and his friend that I made some special meatballs just for them, no charge."

After Ashley delivered the sauce and the message, Tony said, "See, boss, this place sure knows how to treat its customers!"

For the next ten minutes, Tony and the boss drank wine and managed to finish the plate of breadsticks and sauce. In the interest of keeping the peace, they kept the conversation to a minimum.

The boss yawned. "I must stop drinking this wine. It's making me a little tired."

Tony yawned back, "Yeah, me too." He yelled again to the kitchen: "Better bring us dem meatballs while we're still awake!"

CHAPTER THIRTY-FOUR

It was dark, damp, and scary. Adam groped for a light switch but found none. He turned around and tried walking up the stairs, but only succeeded in hitting his head on a low-hanging beam. The noise from the refrigerator motors drowned out his screams for help. He kept asking himself, *Why is this happening to me?* Sitting on the floor, he put his hands across his eyes and tried to hold back the tears.

It seemed like forever before the wooden trapdoor opened. Because of the backlighting, Adam couldn't see who was walking down the steps, but he assumed it was Aldo. Whoever it was, the person was holding a small flashlight.

"Why did you trap me in the basement?" he asked.

As Adam stared at the silhouette of the man, he realized that it wasn't Aldo. It took a few seconds for his eyes to grow accustomed to the dim light. He couldn't believe it; before him stood the old man. It dawned on Adam that all hope was lost. The old man grabbed him by the shoulder and pushed him forward until Adam bumped into a chair.

"Sit down and be quiet!" he demanded.

A minute later the room was bathed in light. As Adam's eyes adjusted, he began to look around. He found that he wasn't the only person sitting in a chair. No more than ten feet away sat his friends Anthony and Gina. Their hands were tied and their mouths were gagged, but Adam didn't care; they were alive.

"I bet you are wondering what is going on around here," the old man said.

Adam was so nervous he could barely speak. "Y-Y-Y-Y-Yes, sir."

"You think that you and your friends are going to die, don't you?"

"Yes, sir."

"I told your friends that things were going to change once you arrived."

Adam was too scared to ask any questions.

The man looked at Adam and smiled. "Let me tell you a little story. It started at the high school a little over a month ago. A boy was found doing drugs in the bathroom. Now, you're probably asking yourself, what does that have to do with you? Well, the person who found that boy was your mother. She couldn't let it go. The kid was a good kid, but like many good kids, he made mistakes. She didn't want to ruin his life; she just wanted to know who was selling drugs at the school. As you know, your mother can be pretty persuasive. She was relentless, and the boy finally gave her a name. That's when she told me."

Adam was very confused. Why would his mother tell an old man about a boy doing drugs? Was this old man a friend of his mother's? She had never introduced him to Adam.

The man continued, "I did some investigating and found a disturbing fact: the supplier of these drugs is not an individual as originally thought. No, this supplier is an organization whose business includes that of murder, arson, and other heinous crimes. This organization is run by a dangerous crime boss whose only interest is money, regardless of the consequences!"

Adam wondered whether the old man was talking about the guy with the big, ugly nose. He was still confused about the old man. *Who is this guy?*

"Apparently, this crime boss thought that Huntingdon High would be a perfect outlet for drugs. He had to be stopped. This was a dangerous man with powerful connections. He was capable of eliminating anyone who crossed his path. Catching him required a plan, but it was not a plan without danger. If he found out my true identity, it would have put you and your mother at risk. That's why you had to leave that night. It was all in the note."

"The note?" Adam asked. "What note?"

"The note that I gave you."

Adam thought hard, yet he couldn't remember this man ever giving him a note. "Listen, I never met you before. I don't know who you are, and I certainly would remember it if you had given me a note."

"Actually, you know me better than you think. And as far as the note goes…" he reached over and touched the back of Adam's pants, "I put it right here in your back pocket!"

To Adam's surprise, the old man took off his glasses, his white wig, and his bushy eyebrows. He stood up straight and smiled.

"Dad?" Adam cried out.

"Yes, son, it's me!"

Adam was in total shock. His lips quivered and his eyes watered. His father was alive! He jumped up and hugged his father tighter than he ever had in his entire life.

"You're alive!" he screamed. "I can't believe it. I thought you were dead!"

"That's exactly what I wanted everyone to think," his father explained. "I wanted them to think that you were dead also. As long as you were *dead*, the crime boss couldn't hurt you. I explained it all in the note I gave you. Didn't you read it?"

"No, I never got a chance to read it. Ginger ate it!"

"Who's Ginger?"

"Anthony's stupid dog."

Adam's father now began to understand why Adam had never shown up at the designated location. "But the note specifically said that you weren't supposed to go to your friend's house."

Adam looked at him sheepishly. "Well, I didn't read that part until after I was at Anthony's house, and then the dog ate the rest. I guess I'm stupid!"

Adam's father gave him a big hug and then looked at him straight in the eye.

"You're far from stupid, son. You were on your own, alone, scared, with bad people chasing after you—and you survived! I don't know how you did it, but you even managed to find your friends, whom I, by the way, had to kidnap to protect them. I'm proud of you, son!"

He kissed Adam on the forehead. "I have one question, son. How did you do it?"

Adam smiled. There was a twinkle in his eyes as he replied, "Dad, you're not the only one with secrets, and I guess you're not the only detective in the family."

"Touché!" his father replied. "What do you say we untie your friends and get out of here?"

"Sounds like a plan to me," Adam returned.

Adam pulled apart the knots that held his two best friends, but took his time with their gags. "You know, Dad, I think I like them better when they can't talk."

His father laughed. Gina and Anthony didn't see the humor.

"I can't believe you did that to us," they yelled simultaneously at Adam's dad.

"You two kids have no idea how much danger you were in. When Tony the Match realized that Adam might have survived the fire, he began to search for Adam's closest friends. Once you were found and captured, you would have been tortured until you revealed Adam's location. I'm truly sorry that you were inconvenienced, but by taking you off the streets, I saved your lives."

As Adam, his father, and his friends took to the stairs, there were still some unanswered questions.

"Dad, the bad guys are still out there. Aren't we still in danger?"

"I don't think so," his father replied.

"But what will we do if they capture us?"

"I don't think that they are capable of capturing anyone at this moment."

Aldo greeted them as they emerged from beneath the sink. He winked at Adam and said, "Basement is like treasure chest: full of many good things!"

Adam smiled but was still puzzled by his father's reply. There still remained some questions that were haunting him. As they walked through the kitchen, they were joined by Ashley and the little old lady. Aldo peered through the kitchen door's diamond-shaped glass. Happy with what he saw in the dining room, he beckoned everyone to follow.

Sitting at the far booth in the corner were Tony and his boss. Each of their heads was face down in a bowl of meatballs. Red sauce dripped from their hair, their faces, and their custom-designed suits. Ashley, the dancing waitress, was quite pleased.

"What happened to them?" Adam asked.

"They were drugged," his father replied.

"Drugged by whom?"

"I did it," the little old lady replied. "I made my special meatballs and sauce, just for them."

Adam stared at the lady. She looked innocent enough. "Who are you?" he asked.

The woman had a broad smile on her face. "What's the matter, Adam? Don't you recognize your own…,"—she pulled off her granny glasses, her wig, and her false nose—"mother?"

Adam no longer cared about being cool in front of his friends. He grabbed his mom, kissed her, and cried. "I love you," he kept saying. Over and over again, "I love you." It was contagious. Soon everyone was crying—even Aldo.

Chapter Thirty-Five

Adam's father directed his wife to lock the doors of the restaurant and asked her to stay in the dining room to watch over the sleeping gangsters. He then gathered everyone else back into the kitchen and had them huddle around him. Speaking in just above a whisper, he explained the final part of his plan.

"What I'm about to say requires that you keep a secret. Can I trust you?"

They all nodded their heads.

"As I told you before, those two gangsters are very dangerous men. The police have known about them for years but have never been able to convict them of any crimes. If my plan works, they will be in jail for a very long time."

He turned to Adam. "I need your Gameboy."

"My Gameboy? Isn't this a bad time to start playing video games?"

"Yeah, his Gameboy doesn't even work!" Anthony chimed in.

Adam's dad turned to Anthony and asked, "How do you know about his Gameboy?"

"He kinda gave it to me."

"I didn't give it to you, you took it!" Adam shouted.

Adam's father put his finger to his lips. "Quiet down, you two. I have to think for a minute."

They all waited, wondering about the Gameboy. Adam thought his father had gone into a trance, but within a minute he removed his finger from his lips and spoke.

"First of all, the Gameboy is not broken."

"Yes, it is!" Anthony stated. "I put in new batteries, and it still won't work."

"That's because you don't know the code."

"What code?" Adam asked.

"The code to release the data that I stored in the cartridge."

Adam had no idea that his father knew anything about computers, yet he was talking about secret codes and data that he had managed to store in his Gameboy. He had to ask, "Dad are you some kind of secret agent or something?"

His father laughed. "Do you think that you're the only one who knows about computers? I've done some hacking in my younger years."

"You're a hacker?" Adam asked in disbelief. He turned to Anthony and Gina and proudly stated, "My dad's a hacker!"

"Well, I wouldn't go quite that far," his dad explained, "but I did manage to secretly store information in the Gameboy."

"What kind of information?" Anthony asked.

Adam's father took a deep breath. "You see, when Adam's mom came to me about the drug problem and I discovered who was behind it, I knew that I was going to have to go undercover. I became Mr. Irving, the old man. Posing as an accountant, I secured a job with the crime boss. I never saw him selling drugs, but that didn't matter. It took a while to gain his trust, but I managed to get the records of all his drug-trafficking transactions. The man has made millions; more than enough to put him in jail. I stored all his accounting bookwork in the Gameboy."

"How can making millions of dollars put him in jail?" Adam asked.

"Yeah, especially if you never saw him selling drugs," Anthony added.

Adam's father smiled. "That's the beautiful thing about my plan. He can be sent to jail even though it can't be proven that he sells drugs."

"How?" both boys asked.

"Income tax evasion, that's how! He never paid taxes on the money he made. He made the same mistake that put Al Capone in jail for twenty years."

"Who's Al Capone?" Anthony asked.

"You know," Adam's father rattled off, "Mr. Big, Elliot Ness, the G-men, the Untouchables."

The boys looked at him as if he were speaking another language.

"Never mind, it's not important. What's important is that we get the Gameboy and give it to the police. You know what's ironic? The boss actually gave me permission to plan the next twenty years of his life. I'm just doing what he asked!"

"But what about the guy with the big nose? Is he going to jail for income tax evasion?" Gina asked.

"I'm afraid not," Adam's father replied. "I had to think of something else for Mr. Tony the Match. He may not look it, but he's a very smart arsonist. For the last twenty years, he has gotten away with setting hundreds of fire. That's why I set him up."

"You set him up? How?" Gina asked.

"You see, Tony was hired by the boss. The boss learned the location of the house belonging to the teacher who caught the boy doing drugs. He also knew that she was married to a police detective. That's why he sent Tony to kill the occupants by burning the house down. As Mr. Irving, I found out about it and let it happen. But minutes before, I managed to get Adam and his mom out of the house. I then snuck around the back and took this."

He showed everyone a picture of Tony lighting the fire.

"This picture proves that Tony was responsible for killing three people."

"But he didn't kill you," Gina added.

Adam's father put his finger back to his lips. "Shhh. That's the secret you all must keep for the rest of your lives."

They then realized the genius of his plan.

"If we remain dead, Tony goes to jail for life!"

Adam's dad handed the picture to Gina. "Make sure Anthony gives this over to the police."

"Why don't you give it to the police yourself?" Anthony asked. As soon as the words escaped his lips, he realized that Adam and his parents had ceased to exist in Huntingdon Valley. Saddled with the new responsibilities that had been handed to him and the realization that he would probably never see his best friend again, he hugged Adam and said, "This place won't be the same without you."

Again Adam was overcome with emotion. In the coolest fashion he could muster, he replied, "Do me a favor?"

"I'll do anything you ask," Anthony responded. "Just name it."

"Make sure Gina doesn't get zits!" Adam said with a grin.

Everybody broke into laughter, all except Gina. She slugged him so hard that, once again, there were tears in Adam's eyes.

CHAPTER THIRTY-SIX

As the siren in the distance grew louder, Aldo, Ashley, Gina, and Anthony went into the dining room, while Adam and his parents left through the rear kitchen door. Tony and his boss were still sleeping at the booth with their heads immersed in their food.

"Should we wake them?" Gina asked.

"I don't think so. It seems that they are really enjoying the sauce," Ashley replied in a perky voice.

The siren sound grew very loud and then stopped in front of the restaurant. A moment later, Detective Tim Faraday entered. He saw Aldo and his entourage standing in the middle of the restaurant. "What's going on here?" he asked.

In unison, they all pointed to the booth and said, "Arrest them!"

Faraday looked at the two men who were beginning to awaken. They were a mess.

"Arrest them for what? Poor eating habits?"

"No," Aldo stated, "for murder and dealing drugs!"

"Do you have any proof that would substantiate that allegation?"

Aldo put his hands on Anthony's shoulders. "I don't, but this young hero does. He solved the biggest crime in Huntingdon Valley."

Anthony looked at Aldo. "I did?" Aldo smiled and nodded. Anthony nodded back. "Oh yeah," he said, "I did!" He handed the picture to Detective Faraday. "And I have more evidence at home."

The picture was exactly what Faraday needed. He walked over to the groggy gangsters and placed them in handcuffs.

The boss opened his eyes, and with red sauce dripping from his face, he asked, "What happened? What's going on?"

Aldo smiled and simply replied, "Man who sell drugs to children should taste own medicine!"

EPILOGUE

One night, four months later, the phone rang.

"Hello?"

"Hey, hero, how's it goin'?"

"Adam?" Anthony asked with excitement in his voice.

"Shhh, Adam's dead, remember?"

"Oh yeah. Hey, I just realized I'm speaking to the dead. Neat! Where are you?"

"On a cruise ship. My parents thought we needed a little vacation."

"Cool!" Anthony replied. "Hey, tell your dad thanks."

"Thanks for what?"

"The bike."

"What bike?"

"The bike that he bought me to replace the one you wrecked."

"My father didn't buy you a bike."

"Yes, he did. It came a few weeks ago. A bright red new BMX."

"You're crazy. I'm telling you that my father never bought you a bike!"

"Are you sure?'

"I'm positive! Did it come with a note?"

"Yeah. Your father used one of his phony names. The note said, 'Here's a little present that I know you need,' signed Nick."

There was complete silence on the phone.

"Adam, are you still there?"

"Yes, I'm here, Anthony. Listen, Anthony, I forgot to tell you something."

"What did you forget to tell me?"

"It's about your library card."

"My library card? What about it?"

"I think I gave it to Santa Claus!"

ACKNOWLEDGMENTS

I would like to thank my beautiful wife, who gave me the confidence to write my story and put up with all my crazy ideas. Thanks to my friend Dina, who offered her advice and editing skills in the early stages. Kudos to my final editor, Earl, who showed me how to make *The Chase* even better. Finally, I offer my gratitude to those who believed in my dream. Bringing this book to life would not have been possible without the efforts of Dan and all the wonderful people at Indigo River Publishing.